LETTERS FROM
YOUR NIGHTLY NELSON

Written by Nelson May, Charlotte, NC.

Edited by Sharon DiCenzo Gomez.

Cover by Ian Nguyen.

LETTERS
FROM
YOUR
NIGHTLY NELSON

EBOOK ISBN: 9781620955741
HARDCOPY ISBN: 978-0-615-62482-2

For more information on this book you can visit:

www.lettersfromyournightlynelson.com,

www.lfynn.com

and

www.facebook.com/LettersFromYourNightlyNelson.

Acknowledgements:

I want to personally thank my editor, Sharon DiCenzo Gomez, for all of her time and effort put into this book. On or about the time that this book is being published, she should be finishing her master's degree. If you need an editor, I can put you in touch with her. Sharon is also a good, true friend and a wonderful mother.

I would also like to thank my good friend, Ian Nguyen. I have always been able to give Ian a thought or a drawing on a napkin and he never ceases to amaze me. He is a great artist and photographer. If you like this book's cover, let me put you in touch with Ian. Ian's inspiration for the cover was born from a popular painting by Neal Adams. For this, we pay homage to the great Neal Adams.

There once was a little boy who was told that he would never amount to anything.

That little boy was me.

Letters From Your Nightly Nelson

Table of Contents

V. Understanding Men 65

VI. Understanding Women 97

X. Afterthoughts   **185**

Forward

In my career I have tried to write a few books. When I say a few, I mean about eight, but writing a book is not an easy task. I am sure most of you reading this have tried a time or two. Authors make it sound so easy. Write a book, get published and make some money. Well, let me tell you, it doesn't work that way. Writing a book is tough, and it is not for the "easily distracted one". I have tried to write a story on science fiction (I love to read sci-fi by the way). I have tried to write a book on motivation. I guess you could say I wasn't motivated enough. I tried to write a book on how to change your life for the better. I tried to write a book on how to relax. I am pretty good in the film and TV business, and have even tried to write a book on how to edit video in Final Cut Pro. I guess you can infer that I haven't written any of these books.

Let me say this again. Writing a book is tough and that is why people that write books are called authors. They are trained to do this sort of thing. But I found a work-around. In fact, I always find a work-around. I found that if you were passionate enough about a subject, the book would write itself. Well the book wouldn't literally write itself, you still have to do the work.

I found that I had a passion for comedy. I am not a trained comedian, but I have taken a few acting classes and even an improv class. I found out that I could make people laugh. I was like this ever since I can remember. I also come from a family of jokesters. I was never the class clown, but I always had this obtuse sense of humor.

I wonder if I got it from my grandmother. God rest her soul, she was a great woman. She really loosened up when she relocated from Pittsburgh to Florida. My dad says that when you take any person out of Pittsburgh, they are much happier and friendlier.

Anyway, one night when I was home from college, my grandmother was staying with us and she was telling me stories about how she and the other "old bats" wreaked havoc on the retirement town of Sebring, FL. I guess she thought it was her right to be a muddled old woman that did nothing but complain.

Sorry, I was off on a tangent there.

My grandmother told me about a prank caller that woke her up one night. She told me that the caller said some of the most terrible things to her. This made my grandmother mad and she decided to strike back. She said something as equally vile if not worse to the prank caller. The guy said, "Ma'am, that was really good, I've never heard it said that way before. You have a good night." And she told him to have a good night as well.

Comedy is in my blood. As a kid I used to make these fake radio shows with other kids in the neighborhood on my sister's cassette recorder. I never missed an opportunity to "jump on the joke". I feel a joke is wasted if it pops into your mind and you don't use it.

I grew up with a lot of comedic influences. As far back as I can remember, we watched the Carol Burnett show. She was a genius. So was Tim Conway. So was Harvey Korman. I think I had more fun laughing at Harvey Korman trying not to break character while in a scene with Tim Conway. That was comedy. Good clean comedy. When I say clean, I don't mean potty-mouth comedy. I am not against it, but I find it so much funnier when you insinuate sexual innuendos rather than say the word fuck.

It's just funnier.

I guess it is kind of like that Jewish comedy of the 60's where some guy said, "I lost my "schmeckle". Schmeckle wasn't a word, but it sounded funny. Then he would say something like, "You don't know what a schmeckle is? It is like a smchlotch, only bigger!"

Again, I don't condone foul language in comedy, but it was never my thing. I thought Richard Pryor was a genius. Redd Foxx was hilarious. Of course, we all love Bill Cosby. Later, I was introduced to Steven Wright, Bob Nelson and some of the other Rodney Dangerfield-esque comedians. These guys were all very cerebral, and they were funny. They made light of things that happen to us in ordinary everyday life. Seinfeld was the best example of this type of comedy.

I also like smart comedy from Jon Stewart, Daniel Tosh (Tosh.0) and Chelsea Handler. They've all had some sort of influence on the way I think about my world.

I like to watch people--not in a sociopathic sort of way! I pay attention to things that are going on around me. I try to point out the obvious that most of us overlook and let you know how funny it is. That is my kind of humor. That is the way I think and the way I write. I am really off the wall. As I said before, I think very obtusely. That is how I see the world.

So back to me.

You do know this book is about me.

After college I never did anything with my biology degree, except try to teach for a few months and that was horrible. After many radio and TV jobs, I finally had the idea to try to produce and air a thirty-minute comedy talk show like Dave Letterman. *Nelson at Nite* was born. It was short-lived; only a few episodes, but I pulled it off. And compared to some of the other stuff that was on cable access, it was pretty good. Well, some of it was. Comedy is so hit or miss because something that you may think is funny can bring dead silence to an audience.

Anyway, you learn and refine and hope people laugh. From there I started doing *Nelson at Nite* in my home and putting it on Facebook and YouTube. It was getting good results, but again, this was an experiment and just fun for a bunch of out of work crew and actors. Before Facebook came out there was this social webpage called MySpace. You might remember it. At the time it was the heat. You could also write blogs. Yes, blogs.

I had something there. I started to write or blog all the weird stuff that was floating around in my head. It was fun. My friends were reading it and making comments.

It was a good run, but then came Facebook. The horror. The humanity. MySpace was no more, and you couldn't blog on Facebook. I was done for a while, until I discovered the podcast. Well it was always around; I just didn't know I could use it for the blogs. From there, I decided to film my blogs and put them up in video form.

I hope that most of my ideas are original. With so many people out there writing comedy, ideas have to cross. The other thing that makes original ideas more difficult is that we are surrounded by so much media via the TV and the Internet. I hope I didn't hear an idea in passing and it jumped up from my subconscious mind when I was writing.

In closing, I have to give credit to a few friends. Some of these themes have come from discussions and through the help of friends. I want to thank my best friend (Jevon Thomas) for helping me record *1-800-TALK-SHIT*, which led to so many good ideas. Thanks to my friend Mark Sanders whose off the wall writing led to a few of my blogs. Also, thanks go out to my razor-sharp friend Steve Molnar; he came up with a few zingers. There are a few other people who don't want me to publish their names, so I thank you all from the bottom of my heart.

And finally, I appreciate my friend Gail Sanders who has been a silent sounding board for all of my crazy ideas.

I hope you enjoy
Your Nightly Nelson,

and remember to

GET YOUR
NIGHTLY NELSON ON!

Letters From Your Nightly Nelson

1. Science, Physics, Mathematics and the Universe

The Ultimate Pickup Line

This is a letter from Your Nightly Nelson giving the world The Ultimate Pickup Line:

For a man, starting a conversation with a woman can be quite difficult. So in turn, the male gender has resorted to a "line" or "pickup line". Yes you know them all. "Do you come here often? Didn't I see you at the market last week?" and so on.

If you are a woman I am sure you've heard them all too. Using transcendental meditation in conjunction with my private think-tank housed in an undisclosed location, I now give to the men of the world: The Ultimate Pickup Line.

Here you go. This one will work every time. Walk up to a woman and say,

"Hi my name is Nelson, and I can be changed."

Bam!

When you see her reaction you will wonder how you weren't able to live without the phrase: "I can be changed."

What woman **wouldn't** want you?

This is what women want.

This is **what** they live for! Nothing more than to change a man into what **they** think **he** should be. You are now putty in her hands. She can reshape you. She can remold you.

So the next time you want to meet a woman, use The Ultimate Pickup Line.

This is a letter from Your Nightly Nelson.

Why Movies
Were Invented

This is a letter from Your Nightly Nelson explaining the necessity for motion pictures:

You could say Thomas Edison invented the motion picture, although he really didn't invent the movie camera. He just improved upon it.

According to popular belief, movies are entertainment. In actuality, movies are just another tool for big business to take your money.

Okay, that was a little harsh. There are some really good movies that are worth paying the "big money" to see. Here is the real reason why movies were invented. They were invented to get you out of a bad date.

Yes, to get you out of a bad date.

You are at dinner and things are going so-so. You have to make a decision. You either have to bail out using some pathetic excuse or go on with the night and suffer over drinks.

Help is now available my brave socializer! You can go to a movie.

A movie adds that needed dialogue that was suffering during dinner. It also kills about two hours.

When the credits roll and the lights come on you just yawn and say, "Wow, look at the time. We need to get you home."

There you have it.

An out!

A very good out!

You look good. She looks good. Everyone saves face and you never pick up the phone again.

Bad Date? Suggest a movie.

You'll be happy you did.

This is a letter from Your Nightly Nelson.

White People and Extraterrestrials

This is a letter from Your Nightly Nelson to stupid white people:

White people can be really stupid when it comes to certain situations. Take, for instance Earth's first visit by an extraterrestrial. When a UFO lands, I am certain that a bunch of stupid white people will walk right up to the spacecraft and say something idiotic like, "Maybe we can talk to them or learn something from them."

Meanwhile if there is a black guy anywhere in the vicinity, he has been running full speed and is probably two miles down the road.

Think about it, in all of the reported UFO abductions have you ever heard of a black person being abducted? No. That is because black people know when to get the hell out.

You never see black people getting possessed either. Other than in the movies, they aren't stupid enough to stick around if an evil spirit appears. I quote or paraphrase the late Richard Pryor. During a standup comedy set, he was talking about the movie *The Amityville Horror*. A voice in the movie said "GET OUT". The black guy hauled ass and got out of the house.

In contrast, white people have to stay around and see what happens next. Don't white people have any common sense?

When you are in a cemetery and something starts calling your name while bouncing around on a tombstone, are you going to stand there and look at it? If you're white, chances are you will.

White people will try to make intelligent and/or hopeful statements like, "Maybe it's grandma and she wants to talk to us."

No idiot, it might want to eat your face.

Meanwhile, the black guy is two miles down the road.

It's tough being a Caucasian.

This is a letter from Your Nightly Nelson.

My Three Laws
to Better
Living

This is a letter from Your Nightly Nelson concerning my three laws:

I was reflecting over my life and put together my three personal laws for better living. They may or may not work for you.

1. I'm not compulsive; I just clean things when I am drunk.

I was at a martini bar with my friend Gail and we were getting pretty tanked. For some reason I grabbed a napkin and started to wipe down the bar. I looked at her and said, "I'm not compulsive; I just clean things when I am drunk."

2. I'm just here waiting on a call.

I was with Gail and her boyfriend Jim at an art gallery crawl. We were in a retro store that had an old yellow rotary phone for sale. I said we should buy it, take it into a pub and put it on the bar. When someone asked about the phone I would say, "I'm just here waiting on a call."

3. Let me check the book.

I was at home one evening and entertaining company. I had previously printed out all of my blogs and had them sitting on the coffee table. Someone asked me a question. I turned, smiled, patted the pages and said, "Let me check the book."

I call them laws, although they are just really good one-liners or zingers. I keep my house pretty clean, have a rotary phone and am going to have *Letters From Your Nightly Nelson* printed the size of a Gideon bible so I can keep a copy in my back pocket. When someone asks a question, I will reach into my back pocket and just "pull out the book".

I will also get to say, "Let me check the book."

Yes, I do live better now.

This is a letter from Your Nightly Nelson.

Spigots
and
Faucets

This is a letter from Your Nightly Nelson to engineers that design bathroom fixtures:

I'm all about going green. I'm glad we have water saving spigots and faucets installed in our public facilities. They save water and thus save energy, but the engineers still didn't get the design right.

I haven't been able to figure out the angle, but you have to hold your hand a certain way under the soap dispenser just to get some soap. You may even have to move your hand in and out, side to side or back and forth.

Frustrating!

Now that your hands are all soapy, you can't get the water to come out of the spigot or faucet. While the soap is drying on your hands and burning your skin, you are now quickly moving your hands in and out, side to side or back and forth. For all the calorie burning, all you get are little spurts of water. So, you have to move your hands faster and faster just to get those little spurts of water on different parts of you hands while the soap is drying and burning your skin.

The guy behind you is thinking "What an idiot" but wait until he steps up to the plate.

You now have been able to squeeze enough water out of the spigot or faucet to rinse your hands. What you didn't notice was that your ass was activating the paper towel dispenser with all that moving around.

When you turn for a towel to dry your hands, all the paper is on the bathroom floor.

Frustrating!

Isn't it wonderful that you just happen to be wearing a shirt?

This is a letter from Your Nightly Nelson.

Low T

This is a letter from Your Nightly Nelson exposing Low T:

Low T. What a scam! Low T stands for low testosterone. Who has Low T? Apparently any man over forty according to the late night television commercials. If you haven't had a chance to see one, they start out like this.

"Loss of energy? Don't feel like going out and dancing? Fatigue? You could be a victim of low testosterone!"

It is a medical fact that men over forty start losing their testosterone. That is what getting older does to you. You feel tired. You feel fatigued. You have a loss of energy.

No Crap!

Let me break it down for you. Chances are you work fifty to sixty hours a week. You have children that always need attention. You have to mow the yard on the weekends. Even men with regular testosterone levels are dead tired.

Where did they get this "going dancing" crap?

You can't go dancing. You have to be awake at 5:00 a.m. the next day to help get the kids ready for school. Plus, you have to work for ten to twelve hours. If you are a white man, chances are you can't dance anyway. This is beside the point. You are tired because of life, not low testosterone.

The cure for Low T is hormone therapy.

More Testosterone!

Do you want to have more energy, feel less fatigued and go dancing?

Well, you can't.

And if you take testosterone, you will still be a forty year-old guy that is tired and can't go dancing with an even hairier back and neck.

Let's face it, you have grown up. You are old and tired.

This is a letter from Your Nightly Nelson.

So Where Did You Clock In?

This is a letter from Your Nightly Nelson explaining the phrase, So Where Did You Clock In?:

A few years ago my buddy Pete said to me, "So Where Did You Clock In?" I had to admit, I didn't know what he was talking about. By the way, he also explained to me what a "butterface" was. Please feel free to look up butterface.

Anyway, he explained the phrase "So Where Did You Clock In?" and I was really taken aback. I had to look back over the past twenty-five years to give him an answer. Let's just say I don't want to relive the memories. Thank God there was a lot of alcohol involved and that gives me a high degree of plausible deniability.

When someone asks you, "So Where Did You Clock In?", they are essentially asking, "What was the weight of the heaviest woman you have ever had sex with?" I guess a woman can clock in too, but I think men hold the trophy because men can't say no to sex.

So if you can and want to remember, ask yourself, "Was it a duce, can't fit in coach or first class, or am I still drinking to suppress the memory?"

So Where Did You Clock In?

This is a letter from Your Nightly Nelson.

Know
Thy
Percentages

This is letter from Your Nightly Nelson to those men who still try to beat the system:

Many times in the past I have talked about probability defining the outcome of relationships and hookups. I've been seeing so many rookie mistakes made lately that I am prompted to write and further educate men so that they can achieve a better social life. If you are a man and going into any social situation with a woman, understanding these percentages can help you be less frustrated, and then in turn, you may hate your job a little less on Monday morning.

THE VACATION GIRL:

Going for the out of town girl? Whether you meet her in your home city or when you are on vacation, you have about a 7% chance of this one working out. Think about it, the odds are so against you it is insane. Chances are you have asked for her phone number. Even if she gives you the correct number, how are you going to play this one? Before you give her a call, ask yourself, "Why should she return my call? She lives 700 miles away. She probably gave me her number to get rid of me, and has men chasing her where she lives." Secondly, "Do you have absolutely no game at home that you are willing to travel (time and expenses) to try and get to know this woman?"

Remember the 7% chance!

THE FRIEND ATTEMPT:

This one only works in the movies.

Again, let me repeat:

THIS ONE ONLY WORKS IN THE MOVIES.

This is the "can we be friends" attempt. Dude, the woman is not returning your calls or your text messages, what makes you think she wants to be your friend? This is typical of a man with NGS or Nice Guy Syndrome. See the chapter on *Three Things a Woman Should NEVER Say to a Man*. This attempt has a 9.78% percent chance of working. Here is what a man thinks: if he hangs around this woman long enough as friends, she is eventually going to fall for him. Again, this doesn't work--except in the movies.

Remember the 9.78% chance!

THE DYING RELATIVE:

This works about 4% of the time. The worst thing you can drop on someone you don't know (especially a woman that you like) is the, "I have a sick relative and I just need to talk to help me get though this." Now this is low. You are hitting below the belt or laying on a good kidney punch. If there were a referee around, you would be taken out of the ring.

Remember the 4% chance!

THE BULK EMAIL LIST ATTEMPT:

Now here is a classic ploy that has existed since the mid to later 90's: putting a woman on your joke or party email list. This attempt has a 6.29% success rate. What are you thinking?

She hasn't returned your calls. What makes you think she's even going to read your email? If she does, it is probably a crude joke and you will offend her. And there is no way in hell she is coming to your party.

Remember the 6.92% chance!

Any combination of the above attempts lowers the odds of success by 24.76%.

Here is the equation:

CURRENT ODDS - 24.76%.

For instance if you try to get the out of town girl to call you by saying you have a dying relative, you have really hit close to zero on this one.

You are an idiot!

To recap, I have given you the percentages of success rates in certain social situations. They are low, and if you are stupid enough to play these odds, you deserve to be alone.

This is a letter from Your Nightly Nelson.

Active Darwinism

This is a letter from Your Nightly Nelson promoting Active Darwinism:

Active Darwinism.

I think it's a phrase, or at least it is now since I started using it years ago. The phrase came about while drinking. Everything in *Letters From Your Nightly Nelson* seems to come from one form of drinking or another.

I remember telling my buddy over a Guinness (or six) that we needed some sort of control over stupid people. Now they have rights, just like you and I, but they shouldn't be allowed to have children. Stupid people breed stupid children. This is a dogma that will remain in society until the collapse of mankind.

We need to get these people out of the gene pool. Remember Charles Darwin? He was the scientist that laid the foundation for the theory of evolution. Charles Darwin is the guy that the "right wing" Christians absolutely hate. You know the fight: evolution versus creationism in schools.

Charles Darwin said that the strong will survive and the weak will die off. The strong will pass down their "survival traits or good genes" to their offspring, who will then also survive.

This works with animals and all forms of life. Even though man is an animal, the theory of evolution doesn't really apply to him. No matter what the disaster or situation, we seem to have the ability to survive. Basically the strong smart people as well as the idiots live to produce another generation. In essence, we end up with more idiots putting bad genes back into the gene pool.

Man is the ultimate predator and has no natural enemy to control his population growth. Therefore any human can survive. That is why I believe it is up to mankind to police itself.

This is where Active Darwinism comes into play. We simply shouldn't allow the stupid people to have children. Yes, let the weak go extinct and let the strong survive. How you go about this is your choice, although I condone violence in any form.

You are allowed to carry guns in this country by the way. I say that because I simply have respect for the Second Amendment.

Active Darwinism: for more information check out: www.activedarwinism.com.

This is a letter from Your Nightly Nelson.

The Myth of the Dryer, Beer and CD Gremlin

This is a letter from Your Nightly Nelson demystifying the myth of the dryer, beer and CD gremlin:

Have you ever wondered where that missing sock has gone when you fold a load of laundry? Did you ever wonder where that last beer went when you opened the refrigerator? Did you ever wonder where that CD you have been looking for went when you were certain it was in your car?

Wonder no longer my friend. The N Man and his think-tank have an answer. First of all in case there is any skepticism concerning our results, we want you to know that we have followed the scientific method and found a 0.006% variance in our final data. If that is good enough for *JAMA* (*The Journal of American Medicine*), then that is good enough for us!

Anyway, let me present our results in a form that would be used in presenting any white paper to the scientific community.

First let me review the scientific method:

1. Observe some aspect of the universe.

2. Invent a tentative description, called a hypothesis, which is consistent with what you have observed.

3. Use your hypothesis to make predictions.

4. Test those predictions by experiments or further observations and modify the hypothesis in light of your results.

5. Repeat steps 3 and 4 until there are no discrepancies between theory and experiment and/or observation.

Let's take a look at the experiment:

1. Our observation: We know that every time we open the dryer to fold the laundry, there is always one sock missing. We also know that when we go to the refrigerator for a beer, there never is any. Finally when you are in traffic, and you open the CD jewel box, the CD is never there. You can dig around inside your car and you will never find it.

2. Our hypothesis: Socks, beer and CDs go missing when you need them the most.

3. Our experiment and prediction: We are going to do laundry, put beer in the refrigerator and drive around listening to CDs and we expect them to disappear.

4. Our results: Over the course of many days we have found socks, beer and CDs missing from their respective places. In addition, we installed trans-dimensional micro– UV– IR and Proton cameras in the dryer, the refrigerator and the car.

5. Due to intensive testing and a data variance of no more than 0.006%, we have found that a small gremlin or dwarf is responsible. (Due to limitations in advanced science, we can't determine which species this is because we could not obtain a large enough DNA sample to prove whether the entity was a gremlin or a dwarf.) But for argument's sake, we will deduce that a gremlin steals your socks, drinks your beer and takes your CDs.

There you have it, one of the life's largest questions once again solved by the scientific method.

This is a letter from Your Nightly Nelson.

The
80/20
Rule

This is a letter from Your Nightly Nelson giving new meaning to the 80/20 rule:

From a sales standpoint, the 80/20 rule says that 80% of your sales come from 20% of your clients. Let's apply this rule to dating. If you think dating is tough, this rule will put your heartache into perspective.

If you want to get one date or even two dates, you have to talk to approximately one hundred people. If you are on a dating website, you are going to have to contact one hundred women. Out of these one hundred women whom you contact, twenty are going to talk to you. Out of the twenty, two will go out with you.

Even though you are going to get business from 20% of your clients, it usually boils down to two actual sales.

When I was in sales, that was the way the math worked. Eventually, you will get 20% that you can draw from at any time. Then, you are elevated to super stud.

Until then, you are going to get two women. Or if you are a schmuck, you are not going to get any women at all.

To recap, you have to contact one hundred women, twenty will talk to you, and two will go out with you.

Ladies, this applies to you too, but you have better odds because men are desperate and very rarely can a man say no to a woman.

Also, see the chapter on the One Mile-One Hour Theory.

This is a letter From Your Nightly Nelson.

II. Religion

Catholics, Jews and the Get Out of Jail Free Card

This is a letter from Your Nightly Nelson highlighting the added benefits of being Catholic or Jewish:

For those of you who aren't Catholic, you don't know what you're missing. I know, you say we worship statues and are a bunch of drunks, but there are some benefits. Allow me to discuss two:

1. Confession or Reconciliation:

This is great! Why wait and try to recant on your deathbed when you can get a new soul once a week! And you still don't want to be Catholic? You need more convincing. You can have a party all week long, do insane things and just plain sin. On Saturday you go to the confessional and ask for forgiveness. But, there may be a catch: What if you die during the week? Benefit number two can be your safety net.

2. Purgatory:

Man this is a good one. I hear so many people walking around saying, "I don't believe in Purgatory!" Why not? You can be bad here on earth and if God sends you to Purgatory, you may have to sweep floors for a thousand years, but you eventually get to go to heaven. That is like having an ace up your sleeve to play any time.

Speaking of playing a card, how about The Chosen People or The Jews. They have it the best. They were given a get out of jail free card. Yes, a get out of jail free card. No matter what, God said they were the chosen people and get to go to heaven.

Cool.

So why am I Catholic and taking my chances on Reconciliation and Purgatory?

I don't know.

This is a letter from Your Nightly Nelson

Expansion Religion

This is a letter from Your Nightly Nelson on religious freedom:

I think it is time for an expansion religion. What is an expansion religion? It is analogous to a NBA or NFL expansion team. The league has decided it is time for another team, so it creates one.

Why is it time? Because there are so many people breaking away from churches' doctrine, and are looking for something new. Many denominations are seeing churches break away: Episcopal, Lutheran, Methodist and even Catholic.

So what do these new churches do? They try to keep as much of their former doctrine while adding to their current beliefs. That is going to get confusing with a lot of small fish in a big pond.

As the population grows, so do potential viewers of athletics. This equals more revenue, allowing sports franchises to award an expansion team. Since there are more and more people that want to worship, why not have an expansion religion? In fact, make it the largest expansion since the Protestant Reformation.

Like any franchise, it is going to be touch and go for the first few seasons. But after a few good draft picks and putting together a good coaching staff, the expansion religion should be up and running, winning over sinners and making it to the playoffs.

This is a letter from Your Nightly Nelson.

Let Me
Choose
My Own
God

This is a letter from Your Nightly Nelson concerning the ability to choose our own God:

It's 2012 and I have had about enough from the right-wing "righteous" nut bags trying to impose "their" brand of religion on society. In fact, I grew up Catholic having strong convictions into my early forties. One day, I threw up my hands and just said, "I can't take this anymore." How can all of the sects, denominations and different religions claim that the same God endorses their flavor of worship and everyone else is wrong?

I have found that the "true God" of the right wing nut jobs is just not the God for me. Therefore, I want to be able to choose my own God. We need about four or five Gods to choose from. That way, we can bring in a God and interview him or her. We can ask them questions the way we would ask an insurance agent.

1. What do you cover?
2. Do I have a deductible?
3. Can I have my family covered?
4. Do you cover vacations and short-term catastrophe?

That way we can find the God that fits **our** needs. Competition is a good thing. Remember the breakup of Ma Bell? Once the monopoly was dissolved, telephone rates went down and we got better service from individual phone companies.

They knew they had to treat us well, or we would go to the competition. Every day, cable and satellite providers offer us a better deal to switch over to their service.

I would like to get a letter in the mail from another God offering me a "triple play" plan for one year, and a thirty-day warranty. If you don't like the service you can switch back to your old God.

Gods can even run late-night infomercials like the lawyers and fitness experts do.

Call in the next fifteen minutes and we'll double your answered prayers!

But wait there's more.

If you call in the next 15 minutes and use the code "TV15 Special", you will get free web access to the Perpetual Spinning Ball of Light. Use it to receive grace and goodness twenty-four hours a day, even on your iPhone!

The Greeks and Romans had it right! They had multiple Gods. If one God wasn't working for them, they prayed to another.

Here's a scenario.

Bob:
Thanks for seeing me Aphrodite.

Aphrodite:
No problem Bob. I see you have been a client of Zeus for twenty years. So what brings you to me?

Bob:
Well, Zeus just isn't answering my prayers. He wants more

sacrifices than I can give right now….you know…the recession. Anyway, for the past three years I have been trying to find a better job so that I can keep my house and feed my family. Zeus doesn't seem to be answering my prayers for help.

Aphrodite:
Bob, we can help you. We are running a "get employed in ninety days or your money back" special. But, this offer ends Saturday. Plus we are offering a triple play good for one year. Employment placement + cancer coverage + one office visit with me, in person per quarter. All for only thirty-six sacrifices! That's six less sacrifices than Zeus. And if you aren't happy with my services in thirty days, we can switch you back to Zeus for a small fee of three sacrifices.

Your God just doesn't work any longer. Let's face it, homosexuals need their own God. The current God just doesn't work for them. The liberals need a new God as well.

I'm sure the Wall Street bankers want a money God, but they may already have one.

What do you know? It never hurts to be rich!

If your God isn't there for you, you should have the choice to look for another God.

This is a letter from Your Nightly Nelson.

Thank God
for Breakfast

This is a letter from Your Nightly Nelson addressing the necessity of breakfast:

Men do all the work during traditional-style sex (at least most of it), because we're on top. This can take a lot out of us. Plus, we probably have had a hard day working or cutting the grass.

We are tired. We want sex. Then we want to roll over and go to sleep. We don't want to talk. To take it a step further, we'll give you cuddling, as long as we can fall asleep while doing it.

Why is it that women want to talk after sex? Why do they want to talk about the most intimate details at that time? As I mentioned earlier, men are tired after sex. Our brain is somewhere else.

That's why breakfast was invented.

You can talk things over during breakfast. Breakfast is a wonderful thing. You get a good night's sleep, and then become razor-sharp after a cup of coffee. That's when you can talk. That is when a man can talk. He has his brain back.

Men are rested. Men have caffeine. Men have food in their stomachs. Since we are wide-awake and not ready to fall asleep (like after sex), we listen to you. We will validate your feelings. You will be happier. When a woman is happier, the man is happier and there is peace in the household.

This is a letter from Your Nightly Nelson.

GENESIS 1:26

This is a letter from Your Nightly Nelson explaining The Word:

As I continue with this letter on our environmental series, I give to you The Word. And yes, The Word says that we do own this earth and everything on it. And we can eat meat!

Genesis 1:26 states that he said: Let us make man in my image and likeness and let him have dominion over the fishes of the sea, and the fowls of the air, and the beasts, and the whole Earth, and every creeping creature that moveth upon the Earth.

I have many friends that are vegetarians and there is nothing wrong with that. They are allowed to eat what they want, because this is America and we Americans do what we want. FYI: you can eat meat anytime you please. Genesis 1:26.

You ate meat and your ancestors ate meat. You eat meat, because you can. It is good for you. The Bible says you can eat meat. Going back to Genesis 1:26, a fundamentalist who takes The Bible literally would argue that we **do** rule over the animals and this earthly domain. We can do what we want with the Earth and sky. We are allowed to eat meat!

We can drive energy inefficient cars and use incandescent lighting. Why? Because we can. We are leaving the world to our children, so take all you want.

God made us the ultimate predator. So don't feel bad about eating that steak. Eat it. You're allowed to. Fish? Eat two servings if you like. Chicken? Get an extra box of nuggets, in Styrofoam no less!

Don't recycle and throw out your aluminum cans with the garbage.

You have domain over the animals and Earth.

This letter was written by The Bad Nelson.

This is a letter from Your Nightly Nelson.

God
Does Exist!
Really!

This is a letter from Your Nightly Nelson once and for all proving the existence of God:

For centuries philosophers, clerics and even some agnostics have debated the existence of God. A lot of us are taught about God since our childhood. Others have found him later in life. But every once in a while, we question the existence of God.

A few years ago a Florida State quarterback proved to the world that God does indeed exist. This story was taken from ESPN's website. I will try to make it as brief as possible without losing any of the important information.

The headline read: "Suspended Florida State quarterback Wyatt Sexton was taken to a Tallahassee hospital on Monday evening by local police after causing a disturbance in the street, then identifying himself to police as "God" and "the Son of God".

According to the Tallahassee Police Department report, when an officer responded to a call regarding unusual behavior on Monday evening, he or she found Sexton lying face down in the middle of the street. Witnesses told police that Sexton had been making strange gestures, and at one point jumped onto a car.

When asked to identify himself, the report said that Sexton "yelled that he was God" and acted in a manner irrational enough that the officer pepper-sprayed him.

As police transported him to the hospital, Sexton identified himself as God or the Son of God. By the way, Sexton played in 10 games, completing 55% of his passes (139-of-252) for 1,661 yards with 8 touchdowns and 8 interceptions.

A lot of people criticize contact sports and the integrity of college football. In its defense, college football does have its benefits. It gives men something to look forward to on Saturday, an excuse to continue drinking alcohol from Friday evening into Saturday evening and now has given us the proof we have been searching for: the existence of God.

College football has also indirectly shown that God responds very well to pepper spray.

In the rich tradition of the Mother Church in it's continuation to sell new and improved pardons--Now available, the most popular and best selling can of pepper spray: The Most Holy Blessed Caspian Industrial Strength Pepper Spray. Guaranteed to have your prayers answered effortlessly and efficiently every time.

This is a letter from Your Nightly Nelson.

III. Pets and Animals

Crotch Sniffing Dogs

This is a letter from Your Nightly Nelson to our beloved dog owners:

First of all, let me state for the record that I love all of God's creatures, including dogs. But I ask you to please keep your dog out of my crotch.

One day I was out walking, and in the distance I saw a woman with a very large dog. As we closed in on each other she gave me a friendly hello. Moments later her dog lunged toward me and went for my crotch. I knew that if I moved too fast the dog might perceive me as an aggressive person.

Naturally, I tried to protect the family jewels. So I turned from side to side putting my butt in the face of her dog. It would be a lot easier to walk around with my dignity and half a butt rather than losing the family jewels. I very politely asked her to please refrain her dog. She said it was his way of getting to know me.

I WAS MINDING MY OWN BUSINESS!

I had nothing in common with that dog. Did I invite him over to get to know me?

NO.

Would I want to get to know a stranger's dog?

Not necessarily.

Then again, why would anyone impose their right (via a dog) on to another person, especially in the area (the male crotch) where life matters most?

I respect everyone. When you come over to my house to see my new coffee table I don't put it into your crotch! If I have a bottle of wine that I want to share with you, I don't shove it into your crotch! I don't drive my new car over to your house to show it to you by driving it into your crotch!

So keep your dog out of my crotch.

Let me state a corollary: all animals bite! They have teeth. If they bite their food, then they bite.

Your dog could bite my crotch.

So in closing, please keep your dog away from my crotch. I'd rather lose half of my butt than any of my manhood. Sure it may make sitting a little awkward, but it's better than the alternative.

This is a letter from Your Nightly Nelson.

The
Free Cat
Guarantee

This is a letter from Your Nightly Nelson explaining The Free Cat Guarantee:

I have a cat. Now don't bust on me; cats are mainstream now. They aren't just for lonely single people who live in old apartment buildings across the river in older sections of the city.

Anyway, I now have a $1380.00 cat. I had to take her to the vet because she swallowed over seven feet of thread.

Why would a cat eat that much thread?

Thread doesn't taste that good.

Anyway, I asked my vet that if anything happened to my cat while in her care, do I have The Free Cat Guarantee?

What is The Free Cat Guarantee you ask?

The Free Cat Guarantee is an insurance policy certifying that if you lose your cat while at the hospital; you are given a new free cat. Yes, a free cat. There are so many cats out there in shelters and pounds, why should you pay for one? In fact, why do people even buy cats in the first place? They're free! I think vets should give The Free Cat Guarantee with every visit.

This was a tough ride for me. I was out of town on a film shoot; my parents took my cat to the vet. I am glad my mother insisted that they take her. The vet called me at midnight. I was baked. I had been up since 4:00 a.m. and was helping an AC (assistant camera person) prep a camera. The vet gave me my options. At the time, they didn't sound good. It was very stressful to make the decision that I made.

My parents were really good about this. They watched and fed her around the clock. My cat is now in good health.

Anyhow, I told the story and kudos to all of you that called or asked to see if my cat was okay. Most people without pets don't realize that a pet is part of the family. If someone you know ever has a sick pet or loses a pet, give condolences, not laughter and ridicule.

Maybe having a pet is a good segue way to having a kid. I have gone around the house cat-proofing everything from string to rubber bands.

Anyway, I am a proponent of The Free Cat Guarantee.

This is a letter from Your Nightly Nelson.

Save
The
Chickens

This is a letter from Your Nightly Nelson adding further credibility to the PETA movement:

In December 2011 I was visiting Key West and didn't sleep well my first night on the island. I was kept awake all night by a rooster that was constantly crowing. Wait, don't roosters crow in the morning? This little S.O.B. had me up all night and ruined my day. I told my friend that I was going to go out with a large stick and get us dinner. She informed me that chickens were "protected by law" in Key West.

So much for my week of peace and relaxation.

But, right then and there, I had a revelation. Born out of my spite and hatred toward that rooster was a cure for world hunger. You probably already know that Canadian geese are federally protected in the United States. They poop on public sidewalks, your sidewalk, in your pool and block the road. Canadian geese are a nuisance, and there is nothing you can do about it.

Back to ending world hunger.

I think it's time to lift the federal protection ban on Canadian geese. For that matter, lift it on the chickens in Key West. When someone is out of work and doesn't have any money to buy food, they can go to any pond or sidewalk and get themselves some food.

There you go, food for a family of six with leftovers.

Active Darwinism.

I rest.

This is a letter from Your Nightly Nelson.

The
Wounded
Gazelle
Theory

This is a letter from Your Nightly Nelson to men who need a new strategy on how to meet women:

I grew up with a TV as a babysitter. We didn't have cable in Pittsburgh back in the seventies and eighties. We had an antenna that was on the top of the house. Therefore we got three channels and that one UHF channel out of Steubenville, Ohio. You remember that type of channel. It played all the afternoon cartoons like *The Banana Splits* or *The Benny Hill Show* and *The Paul Hogan Show* at night.

Getting back to watching TV, PBS was somehow in the mix of our four channels and we used to watch Mutual of Omaha's *Wild Kingdom*. Before I even learned to like girls, I learned about The Wounded Gazelle Theory.

Gazelle travel in a herd with both the strong and the weak gazelle mixed within the herd. This makes them stronger in numbers. This also protects a wounded gazelle from predators.

But, lions and tigers have figured out a strategy to put dinner on the table. Predators take a run at the herd, startle it and split it up. The stronger gazelle will usually outrun the predator, but the weaker or wounded ones get left behind.

This is where the predator focuses its attack. Dinner is on the table tonight!

If you are a man and want to meet women, you can apply The Wounded Gazelle Theory to your game.

When you see a group of women, rush the pack. They will split, but the weaker one will get left behind.

This is the one you hit on.

This is a letter from Your Nightly Nelson.

IV. Social Etiquette

The
Dude
Hug

This is a letter from Your Nightly Nelson concerning The Dude Hug:

There is a lot of misconception concerning the proper etiquette of how a man should hug another man. Please allow my infinite wisdom to clear this up for you.

There is a hug called The Dude Hug.

This hug simply says to another dude, "It is good to see you again." Nothing more has to be read into it. It is simply, "Dude, it is good to see you again."

Here is how The Dude Hug works. When you see another man, most of the time you shake his hand. When it's a buddy of yours and you are male bonding then it's okay to apply The Dude Hug.

Instead of a full frontal hug, you place your right shoulder against your buddy's right shoulder: slap him on the back and pull away fast. The quote, unquote "embrace" (for lack of a better word) should be no longer than 0.08 seconds.

Like I said, pull away instantly and make sure there is a distance of at least three feet between you. That way there is no "that guy may be a little too affectionate" awkwardness.

After The Dude Hug it's safe to go on with normal conversation. You can talk about women, football and even buy your buddy a beer.

The Dude Hug applies to all males that are friends or acquaintances.

Here are a few exceptions where The Dude Hug need not apply.

1. Hugging your dad.
2. Hugging your brother.
3. Hugging your uncle.
4. Hugging girls you really like.

This is a letter from Your Nightly Nelson.

This Means You!

This is a letter from Your Nightly Nelson to those who ignore signs:

When you see a sign that says no left turn, who are they talking to? When you see a sign that says have your ticket and ID ready, who do you think they are talking to? When the sign in the supermarket says twelve items or less, to whom are they talking?

This Means You!

Yes, This Means You!

Don't think for a minute that some guy in an airport all of a sudden decided to get up from his desk, take the initiative and make a sign that says, "Have your ID and your ticket ready when you get to the counter", just for the hell of it. Someone made it for you and me. Someone made it so things would be a lot smoother for people like you and me.

Here lies the problem: there is always one tool that gets up to the counter and starts to fumble for his or her ticket and ID. You are also in a slow moving line just knowing that you may miss boarding your flight, all due to the idiot at the counter.

Many times I just want to walk up to the counter and say to that person, "What part of that sign don't you understand? Is it the "ready", the "ID", or the "your" part? What did you miss here? You have had thirty minutes to get these things together. What is your major malfunction? Look at the sign!"

This Means You!

Yes, This Means You!

The sign is not for the woman who made your cappuccino this morning, or the guy driving the taxi that brought you to the airport.

It was meant for you!

When you disregard the This Means You signs, you put a bug in the system. A bug that screws up a well-oiled machine and throws everyone off his or her rhythm.

For example: If you are trying to make a left turn where it says no left turn, chances are I am behind you and you are holding me up. If you have over twelve items in the express line, you are holding me up because I have six items.

So don't hold me up or anyone else for that matter.

When you see a sign that is directed at you:

This Means You!

This is a letter from Your Nightly Nelson.

Just Once
I Want
to be Able
to Say NO

This is a letter from Your Nightly Nelson to all the men in the world that just want the chance to be able to say "NO":

Saying no to sex is virtually impossible for a man. That is why women hold all the power and they can invoke the One Mile-One Hour Theory (see the chapter One Mile-One Hour Theory). Men are powerless when it comes to sex. We like to think we have control, but in essence we have none.

Why can't we say no to sex? Because we don't know when it's coming around again. Remember when you had to wake up at 4:00 a.m. to see Halley's Comet? Why? Because you knew you would never get another chance in your lifetime! Again, men don't know if and when they are going to have sex. We have to be ready for sex at any moment.

It is very one-sided when it comes to the word no. Women say the word no all the time. Men never get to say the word no when it comes to sex, and it kills us. We want to feel empowered just once in our lifetime. We pray for the moment when we can just say no to sex. But the word no will forever elude us.

We just can't say no.

In every situation we are forced to lose our dignity.

Just Once I Want To Be Able To Say No.

This is a letter from Your Nightly Nelson.

Don't Talk
to Me
While I
am at
The Urinal

This is a letter from Your Nightly Nelson, concerning restroom etiquette in the men's room:

I am an easygoing guy. It takes a lot to get me fired up, and even then, I am pretty even-tempered.

I just ask for one thing.

Yes, just one thing.

Please Don't Talk to Me While I Am At The Urinal!

Why you ask? It creeps me out when another man talks to me when I am at a urinal. I don't know if he is being cordial or if it's the alcohol, but no man should try to start a conversation with another man when he is at a urinal.

This is a moment of privacy, a moment of intimacy. When you are at the urinal, you are holding your manhood in your hand. You are standing there minding your own business when a voice says, "It's hard to get a beer around here, don't you think?" Or, "This place is really crowded."

When I am relieving myself, the last thing I want is another man trying to start a meaningless conversation with me. I am in my "safe zone" or my private space. When another man tries to talk to me, it invades that space and I get weirded out!

Men, it isn't cool to talk to a stranger while he is at a urinal.

This is a letter from Your Nightly Nelson.

V. Understanding Men

Please Ladies,
No Innuendos

This is a letter from Your Nightly Nelson highlighting the problem of sexual innuendos around men:

I have said this before and I will say this again.

Men just don't get innuendos.

We get the idea, but when a woman hints and does not speak in 'dude language', we will totally miss what she's trying to say.

Innuendos are a man's biggest problem. You can't walk up to us while we're watching *Monday Night Football* in your new dress and expect a reaction let alone a comment. Now if you are wearing a teddy, lingerie or a thong, you will more than likely get our attention.

Let me say it again, innuendos don't work for us.

Just tell us you want to have sex. Say it. Say it out loud. We hear that. Don't sit there eating oysters or throw us an avocado and expect us to get the hint. There is no fun in that. Just frustration. It doesn't work that way.

You need to say, "Take me now!"

Even though 80% of communication is non-verbal, **stating** your intention out loud gets **our** attention instantly.

Let me give an example. I was sitting at a bar with a female buddy while I was explaining the "anti-innuendo conversation instance". I guess she couldn't hear too well or wanted to see what reaction I would have when she blurted out, "Fuck me now!"

The place went silent.

Talk about getting a man's attention. All the men in the bar were looking at **me**. I could read it on their faces. "This dude is so cool. This dude is one lucky S.O.B. I so wish I could be that dude right now."

Needless to say, after a few congratulatory beers and many slaps on the back, I found myself at demi-god status.

Lesson learned.

Ladies just tell us what you want. Don't make us guess, it will just bring frustration in the henhouse.

This is a letter from Your Nightly Nelson.

Understanding Women

This is a letter from Your Nightly Nelson on how to understand women:

Countless books have been written over the years that claim to give men the ability to understand women. Just like renting a workout DVD, if you have ever purchased one of these books, you have just thrown away a good twenty bucks.

When I was a kid, my dad told me all I needed to know about women. One day, he took me aside and said, "Let me tell you about the birds and the bees." I responded by saying, "Dad, I hang out on the streets and I have a good idea of what you're going to tell me."

He then said, "Let me give you the most valuable information you will ever need to survive on this planet. I am going to tell you how to understand women."

This is what he told me:

1. Whatever you do, it will never be enough.

2. Whatever you think you know, you know nothing.

3. Even when you know you are right, you will always be wrong.

This is a letter from Your Nightly Nelson.

Twelve Steps to Understanding Women

This is a letter from Your Nightly Nelson on how to understand women in twelve steps:

Step one is admitting that you don't understand women and it's better just to go with it rather than to fight it.

Let me get into more detail.

Dude!

You will never understand women!

Does that help? If you are still not convinced then read on.

There are no more steps. Whatever you do, you will never understand women. Even women don't understand women. Men, you need to just say **yes** to her needs and desires, then go on with your life.

This is a letter from Your Nightly Nelson.

Pathetic Men
In Packs

This is a letter from Your Nightly Nelson hoping to help men avoid the pitfalls when trying to meet women:

As promised, I am trying to be an equal-opportunity offender. This time, I am going to give the ladies some shout-outs. Ladies, I'm sure you will agree that you have witnessed the following scenario many times in your social career.

This is something that a woman can see a mile away. I don't know how they sense it, but they can detect it and can effortlessly avoid the Pathetic Men In Packs situation. I have to admit; I have seen this situation first-hand myself. I will tell how I saw it after I explain Pathetic Men In Packs.

Pathetic Men In Packs are packs of two or more men hanging out in a social situation and constantly looking around. They have darting eyes and their body language is saying, "I am looking at you babe and I am getting up my courage to attempt talking to you." Again ladies, you can spot this all the way across a room. Your exact impression is, "My God, can those guys be any more on the hunt for a woman?"

That is just pathetic!

Up until a few years ago, I didn't know this behavior existed in men. I'm sure I engaged in it and probably still do. In fact, I am more than sure. I know when I am doing it.

A while ago, I was on the way to being married. I took myself off the market. I was so content with my fiancée, that I didn't even read the menu.

That's when I had an epiphany.

I saw it.

It was pathetic.

I saw men standing around in packs, eyeing every woman that walked by. I was thinking to myself, "Dudes, take a glance and look away", but these guys just drooled over any woman that was in their field of vision.

I also saw a leader or alpha male in the pack. He was the one to look first. The others just followed suit. The alpha male made an unconscious judgment call for the pack. He thinks, "Damn she is hot!" Or, "Mediocre, but nothing a few beers can't cure." Or, "I would rather have my head sewn to the carpet."

The pack unconsciously picks up on the alpha male's body language and follows suit. Most of the time they all think in unison. For example, "I fear rejection so I am going to wait for the next one, or I'll talk to her in twenty minutes or after the first quarter."

Anyway, it is pathetic; women see through it and run like hell.

This is a letter from Your Nightly Nelson.

Women
and
Blankets

This is a letter from Your Nightly Nelson to women who load up us men with blankets on the bed at night:

As a man, I like to sleep light. Not in the nude light, but I don't require seven covers and a comforter on the bed. There is one thing that always happens when men are in bed with a woman. When she is ready to sleep, she places her feet over the man's feet. We are okay with that until our feet heat up and we have to move them out from under the seven blankets.

Here is another hot topic. A woman snuggles up against the man under these said blankets and said comforter.

I guess I dream of being in a desert or something, but I scream in my sleep and pull all of the covers off my body.

Now I am out in the open air and drenched in sweat. AND, I am freezing. I know I can't go back under the covers because I will burn up, plus I hate sleeping on a wet spot the size of my body.

I'm sure every man has experienced this.

As a consequence, I have to teeter on the edge of the bed, just outside the wet spot, with a corner of the covers draped over my body hoping to dry out while trying to keep warm and get some sleep.

In an hour or two the cycle repeats itself.

Men have no rights even in their own bed.

I stand.

This is a letter from Your Nightly Nelson.

What Men
Really Want

This is a letter from Your Nightly Nelson addressing what men really want:

TO HAVE SEX AND BE LEFT ALONE.

This is a letter from Your Nightly Nelson.

Give
Your Man
a
Blow Job

This is a letter from Your Nightly Nelson on how women can easily get all the things they desire:

It seems that most women hate giving blow jobs. They don't hate them per se. They just don't like to give them. This happens especially after marriage. That is where the blow jobs stop. We as men can never figure out why. We ask, we plead, we do all we can, but that is the one thing you ladies don't like to do.

Ladies, you are always complaining about how you can't get your man to do what you want. Like: help clean up the house, wash the clothes, help take care of the kids, etc. I am going to let you in on a little secret that will get all of your needs and desires met immediately!

Give your man a blow job!

There, I said it and I will say it again.

Give your man a blow job!

Then put a "to do" list in his hands. I guarantee that the garbage will get taken out with enthusiasm. You car will be washed and waxed before you even think to ask. Dishes washed? Foot or back rub? Yes, it will happen.

Give your man a blow job!

Men really want these things. You would be surprised at how much we want a blow job.

Give us a surprise and put a "to do" list in our hands.

You will have your way!

This is a letter from Your Nightly Nelson.

Why Men Spend
So Much Time
in the Bathroom

This is a letter from Your Nightly Nelson trying to explain why men spend so much time in the bathroom:

Most people (mainly women and the children of the family) wonder why the man of the house spends so much time reading in the bathroom. Sitting on the thinker doesn't take a lot of time for most people. But again, the question arises: "Why do men spend so much time in the bathroom?"

Extensive research done by the N Man's think-tank has shown that men aren't necessarily there to read. They are there to get away from the household for a few minutes. Not that we have any dislike for the wife and kids, but the bathroom is man's home base within the household. We are safe there. Men are safe from unwanted conversation, screaming kids and all types of criticism.

Twenty minutes of safety from the world.

Why the bathroom?

Because,

NO ONE IS GOING TO COME IN THERE!

That is why it's safe for men. It's our cave, our haven and a few minutes to read the paper or a magazine without being interrupted.

If you do decide to enter our cave,

YOU DO SO AT YOUR OWN RISK!

If you can get past the watering eyes and overly stimulated olfactory receptors, expect total rejection to any idea, criticism or conversation you want to engage us in.

Yes, this is our space for the next twenty minutes.

Please respect it.

If you do, peace will remain in the household.

This is a letter from Your Nightly Nelson.

Three Things
a Woman
Should
NEVER
Say to a Man

This is a letter from Your Nightly Nelson explaining to women of the world the three things they should never say to a man if they want to keep him:

There are three things that a man doesn't like to hear. Well there are four, counting the word "no", but we will stick to the main three. Let me first mention that if a woman can learn to refrain from these three phrases, she may be able to keep the man she wants a little longer.

First is the dreaded, "Thanks for calling". When we call you on the telephone and have what we think is a decent conversation, you should end the conversation with: "I would like to hear from you soon", or "call me again." When men get the thanks for calling, that is exactly what it means--thanks for calling.

Our mothers, relatives and salespeople say, "Thanks for calling". These three words don't justify affection in any way or the need for men to continue pursuit.

Second is, "Take care". Take care of what? Our health? Drive safely? When you leave to go off to college or the military, your parents say, "Take care". Take care spans a length of time. Not a short length of time, but a potentially long length of time. Or as men see it: infinity.

Last is the most despairing, the, "Oh, he is a nice guy".
Ladies: the last thing you want to give a man is NGS, or Nice
Guy Syndrome. This is a debilitating disease handed out
frequently without the thought of any consequences or
backlash to a man. Polls show that we can handle STDs better
than the loss of our dignity.

Don't worry about sparing our feelings. Just say you aren't
interested. We can take that. Men are used to nightly rejection
as long as it's fair and unbiased. Handing a man a case of
NGS is like hitting him on the head with a baseball bat and
knocking him cold before he gets onto the field.

Do you still not get the concept of NGS? Remember when
you were trying to set up your girlfriend with one of your guy
buddies? You knew going into the situation that it was going
to be a tough sell, so you told him "she was cute".

Cute?

My God what are you trying to do to us? Men do not think in
terms of cute. That is reserved for kids, puppies and kittens. A
good female friend trying to set you up will say her friend is
HOT! Smoking! Incredible body!

Okay, ladies, do you now know what cute means? Therefore
you must know what a nice guy is.

Save us the embarrassment ladies! Just say geek, loser, bad
comb-over or whatever. Please don't give us NGS. I know
nice and good can be synonymous, but used in the wrong
context the word nice can be quite detrimental. If you like us
just say, "He is a good guy."

Good.

Here is the exact definition from Dictionary.com (Unabridged,
version 1.0.1): good; morally excellent; virtuous; righteous;

pious; ex: a good man.

There you have it. The Three Things a Woman Should NEVER Say to a Man.

And of course,

"You aren't watching football this Sunday. We have to go to Home Depot and pick out paint for the garage."

This is a letter from Your Nightly Nelson.

Men
Need
Proper
Prep Time

This is a letter from Your Nightly Nelson explaining the need for proper prep time for men:

It is a well-known fact that a man just can't get anything right with a woman. We can never predict what she wants, so as analytical thinkers, we extrapolate former information into our most recent decision.

For instance, that dress or that hot little pair of pants that zips up in the back? Remember that we said you would look hot in them? We wait and wait for you to get them. We would love to buy them for you, but if you feel they don't look good on you, you will not wear them. And you also will be mad at us for buying the wrong size, thus insulting your body.

This leads into Valentine's Day. Probably the worst holiday for the single individual next to New Year's Eve. It is also the day that men need the most prep time.

What is prep time?

Prep time is the length of time that a man needs to get to know a woman before he can buy her gifts. This holds true for any occasion. As mentioned before, men will screw it up, so we need to know what a woman wants and likes. That way we can't screw up the gift.

Take dating and specifically dating around Valentine's Day. If a man meets a woman in late January, what does he do?

Regardless of what he does, he is boned on this one. If he decides to do something on February 14th that is big and well-thought out, this indicates to a woman that he is head over heels and thus a "spineless yes-man". Other men who do just a little still end up boned, because they are put in the category of men who didn't do enough for Valentine's Day.

This is where prep time is important. Men need a lot of prep time, and I mean a lot of prep time to figure things out. That translates into finding out what a woman wants. A Gartner poll showed that a sampling of six hundred men who asked their women what they wanted still got it wrong because women change their minds constantly.

So men, go for the prep time. Ask for it. When your babe asks, "What are you going to get me this Christmas?" You say, "Sweetheart, I need more time to get to know you, or else I will screw this up. Give me some prep time. Let's try this again next Christmas when I have had some proper prep time."

Proverb: Those who ask, get answers.

This is a letter from Your Nightly Nelson.

Why Men Go to College

This is a letter from Your Nightly Nelson on why men have to go to college:

This letter may be a precursor to the letter, Men Coast After Marriage.

Everything in our daily lives seems to point to sex.

No, not SEX!

Sex in a good way. (Is that all you ever think about? Shame on you!)

Everything men do, every decision that is made eventually boils down to us wanting to have sex. For those of you that absolutely disagree with me, you can substitute "relationship" for "sex". Although not fully interchangeable, you can substitute any word if it makes you feel better.

We have established that everything men do points to attracting the opposite sex. The way men dress, what men do, and how men conduct their daily lives points toward the primal urge we have programmed deep within us: to procreate.

Where is *Letters From Your Nightly Nelson* going with this you ask? Well I am making what is called a literal transition back to the early caveman. And as every woman can attest, men haven't come very far in a few million years. The needs and wants are the same; the times have just changed.

Millions of years ago, a man had to go out and get his woman by either carrying her back to his cave kicking and screaming or just clubbing her over the head to stop that constant nagging, which also hasn't changed a bit over the past few million years.

Man learned that in order for a woman to have his children and propagate his DNA, he had to provide for his woman. (Of course Cro-Magnon man found this out the hard way.) There was competition back then, and there is now. However, modern man has found the solution.

College.

Yes, College.

After many years men soon found out it was a waste of time to do battle over women. Think back to Helen of Troy. The trouble never ended. So man gets smart and finds another way to win a woman.

That is why men go to college. They go to college to get a good job. That good job leads to a cool car and eventually a house. It also helps a man have sex. (That's just a side note: it was a fleeting thought and I wrote it down before it got away.) Women see his cool car, a nice house and say, "I can be a part of that. All I have to do is pop out a few kids and life will be good."

This is a letter from Your Nightly Nelson.

Men Coast After Marriage

This is a letter from Your Nightly Nelson giving men permission to coast after marriage:

A woman gets very upset with her man when he sits back on the couch, enjoys his life and watches football. He still goes to work and mows the lawn, but after the honeymoon he can sit back and say, "There, I did it. I am done."

Why can he say that?

Lets look at some very important factors to support this argument. First, foremost, and by default, men are hunter-gatherers. It is our job to get the food, defend the household and procreate.

Time (just to name one factor) has tried to change us, but deep down inside we still have that genetic imprint of the hunter-gatherer.

Let's move the above argument into modern times.

A man must find a woman, get up the nerve to ask her out, obtain a date, date her for a period of time and finally propose marriage. That is a lot for a guy to accomplish over time with one woman. Not to mention the anxiety that comes with knowing that we will never be able to hunt and gather again. We also foresee that we will be subject to weekends looking at paint samples at Home Depot and aerating the lawn. That is a death sentence for the man of the cave.

So knowing what the future holds and all the work we have to do to Lock In The Trim (see the chapter on The Price for Locking In The Trim), we get to sit back after the wedding and say,

"I'm done. It is finished."

This is a letter from Your Nightly Nelson.

Mr. Wrong
for a
Change

This is a letter from Your Nightly Nelson to all the women looking for Mr. Right:

As I was writing and proofing this book in 2011, I spent a week on vacation in Key West, Florida. I was staying with a friend who was on a dating website. I have to admit that I tried a few dating websites myself with little success. One night we were sitting around having a nightcap and she was seeking her man. She was reading some of the profiles out loud. A lot of the profiles were just awful, especially in her mind. As a man, I had to stop and think. Other than the sleazy line or two, this is how we men write profiles.

We write how we think.

Let's face it, there are fundamental differences in the way men and women think. Men write profiles that are short and to the point. We are of few words. Of course we want love and companionship, but we would never put it in writing for public scrutinization. (This does contradict the chapter on What Men Really Want, but I am going to let you compare and contrast the two chapters.)

Men never hang their feelings out on the proverbial shingle. Even though a woman is dying to read a dating profile with "feelings" the first thing she'll say when she finds it is, "Oh My God, he can't be straight!"

NEXT!

What I am leading up to here is the perception of dating website profiles. Every woman's profile usually says, "Looking for Mr. Right." She is also looking for a man who is compassionate, caring, kind, nurturing and so forth.

Why bother to write any of this. We men will never and can never be held to those standards.

Mr. Right?

When he comes along and he is the one for you, he will be Mr. Right. Even then he will not completely be Mr. Right, and you will have to settle.

So why not look for "Mr. Wrong".

That's right, Mr. Wrong!

You are going to be lucky if you find a man that comes home every night, holds a steady job or isn't a mental health case. You need to lower the bar. There is no such thing as Mr. Right.

Go for Mr. Wrong.

Lets face it ladies, you don't want a nice guy. (Feel free to check out NGS or Nice Guy Syndrome in the chapter, The Three Things a Woman Should NEVER Say to a Man.) Deep down inside you know you want a bad guy. You know you like bad boys. Nice guys aren't any fun. They are "spineless yes-men" who will bore you to death.

Mr. Wrong.

That is who you need to ask for in your profile.

Mr. Wrong.

Try him for a change. At least when you read his profile, you know he's writing the truth.

This is a letter from Your Nightly Nelson.

VI. Understanding Women

Women Talk,
Men Fix

This is a letter from Your Nightly Nelson on why men want to fix and why women want to talk:

This topic has been addressed in so many books. If you've read or have paid money for these books, what you have been reading just substantiates the obvious. Women want to talk and men want to fix things.

When my buddy calls me up and says his computer is broken, he doesn't want to hear, "I'm sorry, I feel your pain." Hell no! He wants me to do something about it.

He wants me to get my butt over there and help him FIX IT!

When I go to my mechanic because my car is broken, I don't want him to pat me on the hand and say, "Hey buddy, I feel for you."

Screw that. FIX MY CAR!

When you get home and your babe tries to tell you about how she burned the roast, you don't want to hear it.

You say, "Order a PIZZA!"

Ladies: just know that you can come to us for anything, and we will give you an answer to your problem. We don't talk. We don't have time. We have stuff to do. We have to move on. There are ball games to watch, we have to mow the lawn, we have to wash the car.

One final note. After sex, we don't want to talk, we are tired. We do most of the work. The last thing we want to do is carry on a conversation after sex. That is why breakfast was invented. (See the chapter Thank God for Breakfast.) We will talk to you then. Let us get a good night's sleep!

Ladies if you want to keep your man, roll over and go to sleep after sex. We will love you for it.

This is a letter from Your Nightly Nelson.

Work
That
Stuff

This is a letter from Your Nightly Nelson to women who need to work it rather than cover it:

As a man, I don't understand women. Actually, most men don't understand women. Even women don't understand women. But, at least I am willing to admit that I don't understand women. That leads me to another topic, please read the chapter Twelve Steps to Understanding Women.

Back to the topic of Work That Stuff.

One evening I was sitting at dinner with a group of friends. There was a lot of talk going on at the table. Let me introduce the J Man. (J. Thomas). He is the other half of *1-800-TALK-SHIT* (a CD we created that covers parenting, relationships and people in general).

The J Man was tired of hearing women complain about having to spend a lot of money at Ann Taylor and Hollister to buy wardrobes. He slapped his hand on the table and said, "Just take some of that money, go to a gym and work that stuff! Nothing looks better on a woman than blue jeans, a t-shirt and a baseball cap!"

The table was startled. At least the women were startled. I was sure they were about to become pissed off.

Anyway, I called the J Man on this comment, and he denied saying it. Next, he added that even if he didn't say it, the comment was likely something he would say. Now I respect that. A man that is willing to say what everyone else is thinking.

So ladies, stand up and take off those clothes.

I mean the expensive ones.

Go to a gym and tighten that body. Men are happy to see you in blue jeans, a t-shirt and a baseball cap.

This is a letter from Your Nightly Nelson.

See The Hill,
Take The Hill

This is a letter from Your Nightly Nelson hoping to empower more women to get up the courage to meet a man:

Ladies: I understand that walking up to a man and starting a conversation with him may be out of place in today's culture. But, if you want equal rights and equal pay, you need to be able to hit on a man with equal intensity.

That leads me to:

SEE THE HILL, TAKE THE HILL.

Going back a few years, I was in a nightclub with a female buddy. She just kept going on and on about how much she liked this guy that was standing across the dance floor. She kept saying how much she wished he would walk over and talk to her. I told her to walk over to him and just say, "Hi."

"Oh hell no!", she said. "That is not appropriate behavior for a single woman in a nightclub. What would people think?"

You know, I just had to throw up my hands and say it. I had to say it because no one else was going to say it. I told her to,

"SEE THE HILL, TAKE THE HILL!"

There, I said it and just for effect I said it again.

"SEE THE HILL, TAKE THE HILL!"

Lookie here girl, if you don't go over to that guy, some other woman eventually will.

Well my buddy stood around and waited for that man to approach her. During that time a woman walked up to that guy and pulled him out onto the dance floor. It was best for me to turn and run rather than face the wrath of a woman scorned.

You know, I work hard. I wash clothes, clean house and also clean the baseboards. I have a lot of crap on my plate. When a female buddy calls me up and asks me how to approach or get some guy to commit to her I just say,

"SEE THE HILL, TAKE THE HILL."

Then I hang up the phone.

I am not going to play pro-con on some situation that can be solved in 30 seconds or less. Not to be insensitive, but men like to fix things and move on. Yes, we have stuff to do. We have to move on quickly. We can't talk all night.

So ladies:

SEE THE HILL, TAKE THE HILL.

If not, I guarantee you will get passed by, you are going to be mad at yourself, AND the other woman for TAKING YOUR HILL!

Thank you ladies.

This is a letter from Your Nightly Nelson.

Why Do You Say He's Gay?

This is a letter from Your Nightly Nelson to women who blame their man troubles on the gay population:

There is one thing that I get tired of hearing from a woman, …well besides no, or I have a headache.

When a man rejects a woman, the first words out of her mouth are, "He must be gay!"

Last week one of my female buddies was, in her words "blown off" by a guy she liked. Now I don't have the whole story. You know there are three sides to a story. Her side, his side and the N Man's side! (If you still haven't caught on I am the N Man.)

Sorry, back to the subject at hand. So my buddy is blown off by a guy she likes and the first thing she says is that he must be gay. Not gay as in the happy type of gay, but gay, gay. I don't know that he is or isn't gay, but considering the real basket case my female buddy can be, I would expect anything to come out of her mouth. Hell, I wouldn't date her either. She even introduced me to the guy and I should have given him a heads up about her. What got into me? Giving a heads up to another guy is the right thing to do.

I humbly apologize to all of the men out there that suffer from the "no heads up syndrome".

Am I on another tangent again?

Back to the subject.

I asked her why she thought he was gay. My buddy didn't have a comeback, she said, "just because."

Just because!

Maybe it was just because he wasn't into you.

Ladies there's a book out there entitled: *He's Just Not That Into You: The No-Excuses Truth to Understanding Guys.* I read the book and it makes sense. Ladies, I am going to save you the $14.93 on Amazon (that total is with the super-saver discount). You just have to say to yourself that the guy just isn't into you. Nothing personal, just say it and mean it!

Now wasn't that easy? I just saved you about fifteen bucks; fifteen bucks that you can use to buy my book, *Letters From Your Nightly Nelson.* Now there is some wisdom.

Do you still think he is gay? Girlfriend, you have to get past this.

Right in that nanosecond where I could fall into full analysis of being rejected, my brain moves on to other issues, like: "What's for dinner?" or "Did the Steelers win last night?"

This is a letter from Your Nightly Nelson.

Women
Dress
for
Other Women

This is a letter from Your Nightly Nelson proving that Women Dress For Other Women:

This is a very strong issue with me, but I have to say it.

Women Dress for Other Women.

There I said it, and I will say it again,

Women Dress for Other Women.

It took a while, but I finally figured it out. Women don't seem to be worried about what a man thinks of their wardrobe. Why? This may shock you. Because it's the way they look at and make comments about other women's wardrobes that matters.

I have dated a lot of women and one agreed with me that Women Dress for Other Women. She confessed that she dressed only for me. That made me very happy.

Here is a litmus test:

1. How many times has a man asked you to wear an outfit or dress, which he likes to see you in so much?

2. How many times have you resisted wearing that said outfit or dress?

3. How many times have you looked at all the other women in the room and criticized what they were wearing?

If you answered yes to any one of the above questions, chances are you dress for other women. Men don't dress for other men. We wear cool stuff to attract women. We could care less about what another man is wearing.

If a dude looks cool and is wearing a really nice suit, we might be inclined to compliment him. This is strictly out of respect-- respect in knowing that guy has the internal coolness to pull it off. But I can tell you beyond a shadow of a doubt, he isn't wearing it for me.

This is a letter from Your Nightly Nelson.

Ladies:
If You Are in a Bar,
You Deserve
To Be Hit On

This is a letter from Your Nightly Nelson to women that frequent bars:

I can't count the number of times my buddies or I have walked up to a woman in a bar, trying to start a conversation, only to be told, "I am here just to talk to my friend."

What!

I'm just here to talk to my friend?

Could you please come up with something better? You can talk to your friend on the phone.

That's why phones were invented. So people can talk to other people without leaving the house. We now have cell phones. You can talk in the car, on the way to your house in which you also have a phone!

What a convenience! Our great-grandparents had to walk eight miles, through hail and snowstorms, over broken glass, past erupting volcanoes just to talk to their neighbor. Many people in third world countries still don't have phones.

So don't tell me you are just here to talk to your friend. You can talk to your friend any time. You are in a bar to be out. To be seen. To meet men. To be social.

No matter what your relationship status, If You Are in a Bar You Deserve To Be Hit On!

Get used to it!

If you're always upset whenever you go to a bar and men won't leave you alone, stay home. My God, most women would kill to have that much attention. If you want to talk to your friend, leave and go home. That way you raise the probability for other available single women that a man can talk to. You also raise the probability of two people having a meaningful relationship.

So if you are a woman and in a bar, you deserve to be hit on.

This is a letter from Your Nightly Nelson.

IT

This is a letter from Your Nightly Nelson concerning the verb substitution of a pronoun (IT):

IT.

Why can't women say the word?

Men say the word all the time. "SEX", yes, SEX! Try it ladies. Say the word SEX out loud. Why do you take a pronoun and make it into a verb? That isn't proper grammar. IT can cover a wide variety of topics for men. IT confuses us. When women are among women discussing the week's activities, they will say something like, "My man and I did IT last night."

IT!

"What is IT?", a man will ask.

Remember ladies, we aren't too bright when it comes to innuendos. If you say to us, "Let's do IT!" And if you wonder why you get that dumb look, it is because we don't understand the phrase, "Let's Do IT!"

So what is IT?

We really don't know. Now if you said: "Let's do the nasty", "get the freaky on", the F word, or just say, "take me now", we would know.

Stop turning IT into it a verb.

IT is converted into verb instead of remaining a pronoun when describing the action. IT can also be turned into a noun when

IT is supposed to be used as a pronoun. We'll talk about that in the next chapter.

Doing IT doesn't tell men anything at all. IT gives us no sense of direction. IT gives us no sense of accomplishment.

When we look at our buddies and say,

"We did IT."

They look at us like we are stupid. They say, "What the hell is IT? Come on man you can do better than that."

So ladies, please use the word SEX within its proper grammatical sentence structure. IT may sound less vulgar, but poorly substituted pronouns do not give proper description to the act.

Tomorrow's letter: why women can't say that other word.

Here is a hint: It's a part of the male reproductive system.

This is a letter from Your Nightly Nelson.

IT Squared
or
IT Redux

This is a letter from Your Nightly Nelson concerning the misuse of IT: AGAIN!

Anyway, you get the picture. This letter is second in a series of the poor use of a pronoun/verb/noun substitution via the word IT for a part of the male gender. In the last chapter we talked about women not being able to say the word SEX (meaning the act of doing so) or any word or phrase describing SEX.

Men are proud and fear nothing, so we give IT a name. Not a pronoun type name. We use a noun! We call "IT" names like: "The Johnson, The Schlong, The Purple-Helmeted Love Warrior", and so forth.

So ladies, why is it so hard to say one of the above or any wonderfully colorful-like nicknames?

They are nouns by the way.

Using the word IT reduces The Johnson down to nothing in our eyes. Again, we men are proud, and we want The Johnson to have proper credit. Credit is due, since The Johnson is the very thing that helps bring new life into our world.

So why can't you say the word? Who told you it was wrong?

Your mother?

Nuns?

The media?

I can't cite one example where someone said it was wrong to say the word.

So ladies, please give The Johnson its proper credit. IT may sound less vulgar, but poorly substituted pronouns do not give proper description to The Johnson. IT can cover a wide variety of topics for men. IT confuses us, especially when you ask us questions about IT.

When women are among women discussing IT, any man in earshot (if he has to hear) will stupidly have to ask, "What is IT?"

Men have respect for "The Other Intelligence".

We are not afraid to discuss a woman's body parts and give them proper names and nicknames.

Why can't you do the same for us?

Please stop using IT!

This is a letter from Your Nightly Nelson.

The
Circle
Of
Friends

This is a letter from Your Nightly Nelson explaining the dreaded Circle Of Friends:

What is The Circle Of Friends? I can tell you it's about as bad as NGS (Nice Guy Syndrome). Well, actually not as bad as NGS, but it's a pretty bad spot to be in for the male ego.

This is the N Man's definition of The Circle Of Friends: a platonic relationship imposed on you by a woman, with no chance in hell of it ever changing.

The reason I am writing about The COF is because I stumbled upon it first-hand and I wanted to warn other men so they wouldn't make my same mistake.

I was chatting up a woman at a party whom I had met a few weeks earlier. I thought I was in. I had already laid the preliminary groundwork the first time we met. When I tried to close the sale, she threw me into The Circle Of Friends. I didn't know what it was. Then she explained it to me. Man I was boned. I knew nothing was happening from here on out. Later that evening, I tried to close the sale again, and got slapped with another case of The COF.

I knew there was no going back. Even worse, all of her friends slapped me with The COF. It was a bad evening, and since it was a small party and I wasn't driving (able to get away), there was little I could do to redeem myself and regain my manhood.

When a woman says no to all of your advances and takes a platonic liking to you, my good man, you have been thrown into The Circle Of Friends.

By the way, life has now completely changed for you. You now get to hear about the guy that hurt her, her time of the month and everything that goes on in her life. You are going to be the closest thing to a gay buddy, even though you are straight. You will even get to hear about the shoes that she just bought. If you have been put into The COF, you are given the honor of being the protector of that woman or group of women, and it just plain sucks because no matter what you do, you ain't getting any.

Can a man ever get out of The Circle Of Friends?

Only in the movies.

I have seen so many screenplays where a guy befriends a girl and they fall in love, or rather she falls for his good guy, quirky habit routine.

No!

No Way!

Hell No!

This will never happen outside of the glistening studios of Hollywood. Once you are in The Circle Of Friends, you're there to stay.

This is a letter from Your Nightly Nelson.

One Mile-One Hour Theory

This is a letter from Your Nightly Nelson explaining the One-Mile One Hour Theory:

This theory was said off the cuff by my friend Steve Molnar one evening when we were out hitting on women.

If there is any woman out there that says she hasn't had sex in long time and can't figure out why, you need to send her to a professional.

Women hold the cards when it comes to sex.

When a woman says she hasn't had sex in a long time, you need to call bull crap! Ladies you can call that on your girlfriends as well.

This leads me to the One Mile-One Hour Theory. Here it is in its most basic terms: Any woman can have sex, within one mile, within one hour of wherever she is, twenty-four hours a day.

One Mile-One Hour.

It's that simple.

Do you know why the One Mile-One Hour Theory works? It works because men can't say no to sex. We can't. Why, because we don't know when it's coming around again. We have to take advantage of our situation.

It can be 3:00 a.m. in a lonely truck stop diner in the middle of Nebraska. A woman can walk up to a man, say the words and he will go.

So ladies, do you still think the One Mile-One Hour Theory doesn't work? Go to the supermarket and pick a man. Any man. Now implement the One Mile-One Hour Theory.

There won't be a problem.

You know he has to say yes.

Yes.

Why? Because men are the hunter-gatherers. You know, propagate the species and all that stuff. It's in our DNA. And we have to say yes, because we just don't know when we're going to get it again.

Ladies you are lucky to have the One Mile-One Hour Theory. Sadly, men don't have this advantage or any theory, let alone a corollary. Our basic window of time is Friday and Saturday night from about 11:00 p.m. until the clubs close. That is a lot of pressure to try to get the freaky on. No wonder we come into work all pissed off on Monday morning.

Ladies, if you have a boss that you don't like, maybe it's because he was shot down. Cut him some slack. We men can't take advantage of the One Mile-One Hour Theory.

This is a letter from Your Nightly Nelson.

VII. Money and Wealth

The Price for Locking In The Trim

This is a letter from Your Nightly Nelson making men aware of The Price for Locking In The Trim:

At some point in a man's life, he will want to Lock In The Trim. This can be via a committed relationship or marriage. As easy as it may sound, Locking In The Trim, requires more than a man ever imagined. In fact, most men don't think about or comprehend the consequences that come with Locking In The Trim.

We all know that you can't get unless you give. This means compromise: a word that most men fear. Compromise means two different things to a man and a woman. When a Man decides to Lock In The Trim, he thinks there will be a little bit of compromising on his part. But, he is always wrong.

The man will pay a big price for his want and need. Another thing he doesn't factor into the equation is that this compromise is retroactive, meaning that it can go back a long way as far as a woman is concerned. It will be thrown on the table with the rest of the cards when it is time to ante up.

So remember men, if you want to Lock In The Trim, you must be prepared to pay the price. Or do as Charlie Sheen does and call on Heidi Fleiss.

This is a letter from Your Nightly Nelson.

What Part
of
FREE!

This is a letter from Your Nightly Nelson wanting to know what part of FREE don't you understand:

I am on a rant. A serious rant! A while ago, I decided to give one of my relaxation CD/MP3 tracks as a download for free. The offer wasn't open-ended and the download wasn't offered forever. I stopped the download at 12:00 p.m. PST to give people on the West Coast a chance to download the track. I posted this giveaway on Facebook, and even sent it out via Twitter.

About an hour later, I was appalled at some of the comments that I was getting about my post. The first comment was, "Why can't you make the download longer than one day? Some of us are at work, and we can't download files."

Christ on a Crutch! What kind of person writes this? Are you an idiot? What part of 12:00 p.m. PST don't you understand? Do you mean to tell me that you are too busy watching trashy late-night reality show reruns and infomercials that you don't have the time to sit at your home computer?

There are reasons you are not allowed to download files at work: malware and viruses! Plus they want you working, not downloading. It is bad enough that you are wasting time on Facebook and Twitter.

How much more of your company's time do you waste surfing the web? If you have time to post a stupid comment between the hours of nine and five, from your job (not your home), you are not working. Why do I know this? Because you posted that you can't download files at work-from work!

If you can get away without working, posting comments, but can't download files at work, don't you have a smartphone in which you can use during lunch to get the download? Better yet, take some of that time that you are not working and call someone who is able to download a file for you. But then you would probably get pissed off when they asked you to drop by with a USB drive to pick it up.

On top of it all, when you got the file, you would find something that you don't like about it. You would then take more time from your job to complain to the company that gave you the FREE file.

There are free apps out there, but when they don't work, I don't complain and criticize the writer. If I have the time, I may just write a short note. It may say, "Thanks for the effort, I know this app is free, but it doesn't work or doesn't work for me. If you make a better version, I would like to try it again."

By the way, while you are not working by posting on Facebook, you are lowering productivity. In January 2012 when I wrote this letter, there was an 8.5% unemployment rate in the United States. While you are messing around on the Internet, not doing your job, and wasting even more time complaining, millions of people are sitting on the sidelines hoping to have your job. Even if they were told that they would not have any Internet access, they would still jump at your job.

FREE!

I understand FREE!

FREE means you get something for nothing.

The next complaint I received was, "The download site wants me to sign up and create an account. I don't want to give out my email."

I have a legitimate service offered at the website www.cdbaby.com/Artist/NelsonMay. That is the only way you can get on their site to download something for free. Again, Christ on a Crutch! (I love to use this term!) Give them your spam email address like a Gmail or a Yahoo address. Give them a fake address!

Remember, the file is FREE!

You people really take the cake. You probably rummage though bulky items like desks and patio umbrellas others throw away only to complain that they are broken or that there is something wrong with them.

Curbside Garbage and Rubbish is FREE!

What part of free don't you understand?

Really, how hard is it for your brain to wrap around the concept of FREE?

FREE, means **you** come get it. If it is FREE on Craigslist, **you** find a way to get it home. If an ad in the paper says it's free, you don't have the right to complain about or criticize the item.

It's FREE!

You people are why I invented the movement called *Active Darwinism*.

Active Darwinism: Don't let stupid people breed!

I agree with the Second Amendment, but I also agree that we should have more gun control. After these two complaints, I am right up there with the NRA. Let anyone have a gun that wants one! Give them two in case one misfires! We need to thin out the herd and take the bad genes out of the gene pool.

FREE!

Seriously, what part of FREE don't you understand?

This is a letter from Your Nightly Nelson.

What Makes a Blockbuster Movie

This is a letter from Your Nightly Nelson giving Hollywood the formula for making a successful blockbuster movie:

Since a television was my babysitter throughout adolescence and my pre-teen years, I feel that I know how to make a blockbuster movie.

Did you ever consider the research that goes into making a movie or a new TV series? I'm not talking about the writing and the pre-production, but the market research. Studios and production companies actually ask people what they want to see in a movie. For certain movies, producers walked around malls in Los Angeles and showed teenage girls pictures of heartthrob actors and let the girls choose the actors.

That may have worked once. But from now on, studios are going to have to consult the N Man.

I know what makes a good movie or TV show. If you apply this simple formula, you will have a blockbuster show.

GOOD SHOW = A DUDE THAT KICKS SOME BUTT + A HOT LOOKING BABE + A HOT LOOKING BABE THAT KICKS SOME BUTT

Above is a formula that works every time. Let me prove my formula by adding the appropriate variables into the equation.

ANY JAMES BOND FILM = JAMES KICKING SOME
SERIOUS BUTT + A HOT LOOKING BABE + THAT HOT
LOOKING BABE KICKS SOME BUTT

Here is a bonus for Bond films. Bond also bags the babe--all
before the opening credits roll!

Wow man! All that and the action continues throughout the
rest of the film. That is what makes a blockbuster movie!

Let's talk about a show that was cancelled: *Star Trek
Enterprise*. Now it was a good show, but it didn't have that
edge. Comparing it to the original series with the legend,
"James Tiberius Kirk", *Enterprise* just wasn't strong
enough. *Star Trek* (the original) rocked. You knew that if you
messed with James T. Kirk, you had a warp ten ass kicking
coming your way. Kirk shot phasers and proton torpedoes first
and asked questions later. He always bagged the babe.
Chances are she was kicking his butt before he bagged her.
(Extra double bonus points!)

GOOD TV SHOW = JAMES KIRK KICKING BUTT + A
HOT LOOKING BABE + A HOT LOOKING BABE
KICKING BUTT

Now let's go to *Enterprise*.

Jonathan Archer was a nice guy (now whether or not he had
NGS, we don't really know). Archer never really kicked any
butt, and there were a few semi good-looking babes, but they
didn't kick any butt. Archer didn't bag any babes either.

OK TV SHOW = DUDE THAT DOESN'T KICK MUCH
BUTT + A SEMI GOOD-LOOKING BABE + A BABE
THAT DOESN'T KICK BUTT

Do you see it in the formula? It adds up doesn't it? Before I close, I want to add a side note. A buddy came up to me a few years ago and told me about the *Tomb Raider* movie (the one based on the video game). He said and I quote, "This is a total guy movie, she has a nice ass, great boobs and all she does is kill people and blow shit up."

Any formula can have different variables. If you do the math, you can change any formula to accommodate the different variables.

For instance, think of all the different formulas that you can convert Isaac Newton's F=ma (force=mass x acceleration) into.

So we have:

KILLER DUDE MOVIE = A SMOKING HOT BABE + THAT SMOKING HOT BABE BLOWS SHIT UP AND KILLS PEOPLE

There you have it: the formula for a successful blockbuster movie or TV show.

This is a letter from Your Nightly Nelson.

The Checking
Account Theory

This is a letter from Your Nightly Nelson helping to end economic woes with The Checking Account Theory:

Have you ever wondered why you don't have enough money in your checking account? Do you feel like you live paycheck to paycheck? Fear no longer my financial pupils, The Checking Account Theory will solve all of your problems.

First let's take a look at a typical checking account. When you look at your statement, you check your balance. This is how much money you have in your checking account. Before I go on, I have to make an analogy so you can fully understand and apply The Checking Account Theory.

We are going to use a simple drinking glass as our model.

The glass can hold only so much liquid. If you are trying to get more liquid into the glass than the glass holds, you are going to have to drink some of that liquid. If this is still not clear, then we can substitute "the liquid" with "alcohol". Yes, alcohol. We can all identify with alcohol. It helps ugly people have sex, raises any level of self-esteem and makes you totally invulnerable to all types of criticism.

When your glass is full of alcohol and you want more alcohol, you need to empty that glass to make room for additional alcohol. Very simple: you drink and more alcohol will come to you.

Let's tie that back to your checking account.

If your checking account has too much money in it, then there is no room for more money to get in. So, for The Checking Account Theory to work properly, you have to spend money. Remember, if your account is full, then there is no room for more money to get in.

So spend. And drink, if you feel you can't spend your money. In fact help other people fill their glasses. That way your account and your glass now have room for more money and alcohol. Don't worry, money and alcohol will flow if you keep good Karma.

If you think you have a problem, please call AA at 1-800-I-DRINK-MYSELF-INTO-STUPIDITY.

Or for money problems, call 1-800-I-CAN'T-CONTROL-MY-SPENDING.

This is a letter from Your Nightly Nelson.

Positive Affirmation Beer Coasters

This is a letter from Your Nightly Nelson giving to the world his new self-esteem marketing tool, Positive Affirmation Beer Coasters:

This idea has been steaming away in my head for over a year now.

Positive Affirmation Beer Coasters.

When you go to a bar you are always given a beer coaster branding an ale, saying Happy Thanksgiving or some other witty phrase. I thought I could print beer coasters that help raise male self-esteem.

They could say, "You are a wonderful guy."

Or for the man with little social self-confidence, "The woman across the bar wants your body."

Here is one for the black out drunk. "Every time you see this message, you are drinking too fast. Slow down and drink some water."

How about a beer coaster that says, "No matter how many times you ask, the bartender is not going to give you her phone number. Please stop trying."

In strip clubs a beer coaster could read, "You are the most handsome, funny and the most interesting guy in the world, until you run out of twenty-dollar bills."

This is a letter from Your Nightly Nelson.

VIII. The Crazy House

OSHA
and
The Porn
Industry

This is a letter from Your Nightly Nelson seeking equal rights for all professions:

I am not into pornography, but I have wondered now and then how this multi billion-dollar industry's infrastructure really operates.

Is there a union? Teamsters? Health benefits? Dental? Optical? 401K? Regulated overtime?

Well who knows? But if OSHA (The Occupational and Safety Health Administration) sets the safety standards for all buildings and structures in the workplace, shouldn't they set standards for the porn industry?

Think about it. Deep down inside, porn actors are people too. Shouldn't they have a fair and safe work environment? So here is what I propose: safety videos for the porn industry.

They could start out like any other safety video.

Imagine establishing a shot of "some type of interaction between co-workers". These co-workers are of course just actors that are in a "mock-up" hazardous work environment.

The voice-over would say "What would happen if you were handcuffed to the bed, and the candle catches the curtains on fire?"

The video would freeze frame. A strong-voiced actor would walk out and say, "Wait, what would **you** do if this happened to you?"

Would you:

A. Scream for help?

B. Try to pull the headboard off the bed?

C. Spit the ice cube out of your mouth and attempt to extinguish the candle before the curtains burst into flames?

The strong-voiced actor would say, "The answer would be C. Spit the ice cube out of your mouth and attempt to extinguish the candle before the curtains burst into flames."

Then, the real scene is played out with option C.

There are many scenarios which also need to be addressed as safety issues.

1. Slipping in the hot tub
2. Slipping on the hot tub tile
3. Falling off the pool table
4. Getting a concussion on the headboard

I feel government-steering committees and OSHA should regulate all industries including the porn industry.

We all know that with proper safety training you can prevent injuries on the job. That would reduce worker's compensation and sky-rocketing health insurance costs. More importantly, it could save lives, maybe your own.

This is a letter from Your Nightly Nelson.

Equality?
Only at
The DMV

This is a letter from Your Nightly Nelson proving that equality can exist in our world:

Dear men and women of the world: I can't tell you the number of times I have heard people ranting about situations that don't promote equality. Religion, race, and class: everyone screams and wants some type of equality.

Now there is an answer.

The DMV.

The Department of Motor Vehicles.

Every state has one and if you are legal driver you have been to one of the department's offices. We all know the routine. Come early. Stand in line. Wait. Find out you have the wrong paperwork. Go to another line. Wait some more. Get called to another section of the DMV to wait some more.

Sound familiar?

No one, and I mean no one, will get preferential treatment. It is the law. You have to stand in line and you have to get your picture taken. No exceptions.

How does this lead to equality?

Think about it. Jack Nicholson has to go to the DMV.

Madonna has to go to the DMV. Even Hillary Clinton has to go to the DMV. Now Lil Wayne may have his posse, BUT he still has to go to the DMV if he wants to drive a motorized vehicle.

At the DMV we are all equal. No Black, White, Hispanic, Catholic, Jew, Muslim, rich, poor, male or female. You have to show proof of insurance. You may have to take an eye test. Maybe even that written test. And finally, a driving test. Then you better have cash or credit. They don't like checks.

Humiliating?

Yes.

A place of equality?

Yes.

This is Your Nightly Nelson proving that there is indeed equality and it can be found, only at the DMV.

This is a letter from Your Nightly Nelson.

I'm Just Here
Waiting
on a Call

This is a letter from Your Nightly Nelson concerning more phone calls:

I was with my friend Gail and her boyfriend Jim at a gallery crawl. We were in a retro store that had an old yellow rotary phone for sale. I picked it up, said we should buy it, take it into a pub and put it on the bar. When someone asked about the phone I would say, "I'm just here waiting on a call."

This is a letter from Your Nightly Nelson.

Who Rents
Workout DVDs?

This is a letter from Your Nightly Nelson to people who rent workout DVDs:

Why do people rent workout/fitness DVDs? Then again, why are fitness DVDs found in video rental stores and kiosks? There are a lot of things in my life that just don't make sense, and this one tops the list.

Take your average DVD rental, four to five bucks depending on which part of the country you live in. You have to take it back in a few days to a week tops, or you start accruing late fees.

Your average workout DVD will claim results in a short time, but come on, that only happens on TV. You can't get rock hard six-pack abs in a week. You can't tighten that butt in a week. You can't lose that thirty pounds of flab in a week to get into that bathing suit. In addition, those of you that actually go out and buy a workout DVD will use it once and shelve it.

So, why rent a workout DVD?

You know you aren't going to use it more than once. What are you thinking?

"Oh, I just wanted to try it out."

TRY IT OUT?

So let me get this straight, for five bucks you want to try it out. Hello, come to the meeting. Think McFly. You can buy it for $19.99 at Wal-Mart.

Come home reality child!

You don't test drive a Volvo, give the salesman $2,000.00 and say, "You know, this just isn't me." Or, you don't drop $14,000.00 to try out a house for a week and say to the realtor, "No thanks, this just isn't what I was looking for."

SO WHY DO YOU RENT WORKOUT DVDs?

Come on. You already know that you aren't going to stick with it. This is America. We don't do anything we don't have to. So why work it away when you can lose it by having liposuction?

Take that five bucks and get a beer. A dessert. Go nuts! Whatever. Life is too short.

So please, don't rent that workout DVD.

This is a letter from Your Nightly Nelson.

Let Me
Check
The Book

This is a letter from Your Nightly Nelson concerning The Great Book:

Let me check the book.

I was at home one evening and entertaining company. I had previously printed out all of my blogs and had them sitting on my coffee table. Someone asked me a question. I turned, smiled, patted the pages and said, "Let me check the book."

I am going to have *Letters From Your Nightly Nelson* printed the size of Gideon bibles so I can keep a copy in my back pocket. When someone asks a question, I will reach into my back pocket and just "pull out the book".

I will also get to say, "Let me check the Book."

This is a letter from Your Nightly Nelson.

IX. Social Science

Niceness Blanketing Technique

This is a letter from Your Nightly Nelson explaining the Niceness Blanketing Technique:

I remember my buddy Steve Molnar saying this while we were drinking at a pool one afternoon.

All men know that meeting women can be tough. We try all the classic methods that usually lead to rejection, but here is a method that brings good results.

It's called the Niceness Blanketing Technique.

The Niceness Blanketing Technique works in all types of situations. Use it at a bar, a party, a coffee shop, a swimming pool, or a gym--the possibilities are endless.

When used properly the Niceness Blanketing Technique will give women the impression that you are a good guy that everyone wants to be around, not the slimy say anything pickup artist that you actually are.

To use the Niceness Blanketing Technique, all you have to do is talk to every woman at the bar, the party or the coffee shop. Be cool and be suave. Don't ask for phone numbers or anything else.

YET!

Let all the women get to know you. Then, you will be the most harmless guy in the room.

That's when you make your move.

Try the Niceness Blanketing Technique; you will be happy you did.

This is a letter from Your Nightly Nelson.

Peace
In The
Household

This is a letter from Your Nightly Nelson on how to obtain Peace In The Household:

For any relationship to work there must be Peace In The Household. What is Peace In The Household? Peace In The Household means that everything is going right for the man. Now it doesn't negate the fact that everything must be going right for the woman.

I lay you out a dogma:

For there to be Peace In The Household, the woman must be happy.

The woman is traditionally the heart of the home; she keeps things running smoothly. If she is upset, then you will not have Peace In The Household.

A man must do whatever is necessary, going above and beyond to keep Peace In The Household. If a man doesn't keep Peace In The Household, then what he most desires (to Lock In The Trim), will not be successful.

So men, don't expect to do the bare minimum to keep Peace In The Household. You have to work to keep Peace In The Household. And you have to work hard. Women keep tabs. You can backslide at any time and lose all the points that you have gained.

No one said it would be easy, but to Lock In The Trim, there must be Peace In The Household.

This is a letter from Your Nightly Nelson.

Fortune
Cookies

I want to introduce to you the very first letter I ever wrote.

One night I was eating in a Chinese restaurant and I opened my fortune cookie. I know you're supposed to read the quotes out loud and at the end, you are supposed to say "in bed". Well it worked another way.

This is a letter from Your Nightly Nelson to Oriental restaurants:

This evening I was eating Chinese sesame chicken. Tradition says that we are to open the fortune cookie and receive a fortune. You also get your lucky lottery numbers on the reverse side of the quote. Good luck, since the odds for winning the lottery are millions to one.

Anyway, I think there should be a paradigm shift within the conventional wisdom pool in which fortunes are derived. Let's say you opened a fortune cookie and it read, "You will see good things come your way."

Crap on that.

We live in a pessimistic society that's still under the umbrella of a great recession. We aren't going to see anything good. All we will see is our maxed out credit card statements and over-drawn bank accounts.

A politically correct fortune cookie should read, "Be on the lookout, your telephone calls are being monitored."

Or,

"You are underpaid and hate your job. Get a new one, but please don't shoot up the office."

How about,

"As you get older, more things will go wrong with your body and you will pay higher insurance premiums."

Now that is honesty.

I want a fortune cookie that feels my pain like, "The price of gasoline will forever climb higher and higher."

You could even use fortune cookies to aid in the recovery of someone suffering from depression.

For instance, "Don't forget to take your medication before you go to bed."

Or,

"Shake it off man. You think you have problems? There are starving children in Somalia."

Better yet, you are sitting alone at night, have been drinking and were too drunk to drive and get food. Chinese restaurants could target the self-medicated with,

"Stop whining and crying. So you got dumped. It isn't the end of the world. Get back on the horse." When you turn over the little piece of paper, the message continues, "We all get dumped, deal with it."

No numbers, just honesty.

Finally for the schizophrenic, you could have a fortune that says,

"There is only one internal voice that you are hearing while you read this fortune. That is Good! All is Good. It is your voice. Just in case, please stay on your medication."

This is a letter from Your Nightly Nelson.

Go Ahead,
Stare
at
My Girlfriend

This is a letter from Your Nightly Nelson to men who have a hot girlfriend and are proud that other men stare at her:

Have you ever wondered why women get mad when another woman looks at her man? If you are a woman, you know why. If you are a man, you have no clue. But as a man you will catch hell later on when your girl tells you that she doesn't like other women looking at you. That is a problem I can't address in this book.

Anyway, a few years ago, I dated one of the hottest women in the city. When we were out, men stared at her left and right. In fact, I couldn't go to the bar and get a drink without a man trying to hit on her while I was away. That made me feel good! In addition to having a wonderful woman, she was also appreciated by my peers.

When I saw a man staring at her, I just thought to myself, "Enjoy the look, because I am going to be hitting that later tonight."

In fact, I mentally encouraged men to stare at my girlfriend.

Where is this entire thing going?

I have no idea, but I had a hot girlfriend that men stared at.

To add a note, a guy once walked up to me and told me I had no right to have such a good looking woman. My reply was: "I want you to look at her and stare. I want you to burn a picture of her into your mind. So later on this evening, when you go home with your hand, I will be hitting that stuff and you won't. Have a nice evening."

This is a letter from Your Nightly Nelson.

The Audacity of Dating

This is a letter from your Nightly Nelson on the audacity of dating websites:

I was answering a few messages on Facebook and all these dating advertisements popped up on the right side of my page. They must think I'm desperate. Well, they're right.

No seriously, anyone can still go to a bar or supermarket and meet someone. Therefore why should you have to pay? Add up the money over time and you could have a decent hooker or gigolo.

In this letter, we make fun of all the different dating websites that are being marketed to you. Let's take a look at a few.

How about:

www.landing.singles.net,
www.blackpeoplemeet.com,
www.christianmingle.com,
www.true.com,
www.smartdate.com,
www.seniorpeople.com,
www.speeddate.com,
www.fitnesssingles.com,
or www.mate1.com.

The list is endless.

Since I'm always thinking, this got me thinking. I need to start some dating sites just to make extra money.

Here are some ideas:

www.maturematuresingles.com,
www.evenmorematuresingles.com,
www.lowaltitudeskydivingsingles.com,
www.bipolarscubadivingsingles.com,
www.lowerIQsingles.com,
www.½Asian¼Hispanic¼Americansingles.com,
www.racistwhitebreadwhitesingles.com,
www.oldercougar.com,
www.slightlyoldercougar.com,
www.slightlylessyoungercougar.com,
www.yourmothercanbeacougar.com.

Or,

www.Iamfinanciallybrokesingles.com,
www.singlesthatliveintheirparentsbasement.com,
www.singleswith3ormoreSTDs.com,
www.takeyourpictureinfrontofamirrorwithyoursmartphone
becauseyouaretoostupidtohaveafriendtakeoneforyou.com.

I can go on forever. The point is these sites are here to take your money. So, get out of the house, walk down the street and meet someone.

This is a letter from Your Nightly Nelson.

Phone
Conversations

This is a letter from Your Nightly Nelson pointing out the differences in phone conversations between men and women:

Most of us have never noticed this, but phone conversations between two men and between two women are two totally different things. Rather than go into a lengthy explanation as to why and how, I am going to use scripted dialogue to explain my point.

The following conversation is fictional and does not depict any person(s) living or dead. We will use Bob and John, and Julie and Laura.

BOB:
What's up John?

JOHN:
Not much. What time tonight?

BOB:
8:00 p.m. at the Firehouse.

JOHN:
Cool!

-Total Elapsed Time (including dial tone): 26.7 seconds

JULIE:
Hey Girl.

LAURA:
Hey Girl

JULIE:
What's been going on since yesterday?

LAURA:
Well, I hated the way my hair looked in the morning, so I started all over again, which made me late for work...oh I hate that guy Brian that always tries to flirt with me in the break room...oh, did I say I saw this cute guy in traffic and he smiled at me?...I'll bet he will ask for my cell number...I hope he has nice handwriting...I don't think I could marry a guy with bad handwriting. Oh, that Brian is just a jerk, then my boss told me I had meet another sales goal this week...

JULIE:
Aw baby...I tried this new nail polish and the guy at work that I have been flirting with didn't even notice.

-30 minutes later

LAURA:
So where do you want to go tonight?

JULIE:
Oh I don't know, how about Bradley's?

LAURA:
Yuck! That weird guy hangs out there who always hits on me.

-14 minutes later

JULIE:
So what are you wearing?

LAURA:
That blue skirt with the white blouse.

JULIE:
Oh no, I was going to wear a blue skirt. But, I can wear jeans.
I am going to have to change my hair.

-12 minutes later

LAURA:
Ok, we'll get there around ten, but don't you dare go in
without me.

-Total Elapsed Time: Who knows.

So there you have it. This is just to prove a point. The
conversation was just ad-libbed to show length.

This is a letter from Your Nightly Nelson.

Let's
Be
Friends

This is a letter from Your Nightly Nelson to single people:

Both sexes get this a lot: the dreaded, "Let's Be Friends".

The question is: should we take this as a compliment or an insult? The N Man says insult. Most of us just move on when we hear, "Let's Be Friends".

Contrary to popular belief, "Let's Be Friends", is not as bad as hearing, "He is a Nice Guy", or "She is Cute".

Just say you don't like us. We can take it. In fact, we respect you for your honesty. Don't worry about hurting any more feelings, because we've been stomped on pretty good already.

Here is Your Nightly Nelson's rebuttal to the phrase, "Let's Be Friends".

"Why, I have enough friends. I can't keep up with the ones I have, and you want to be another one? What could you possibly offer me that my current friends cannot?"

This is a letter from Your Nightly Nelson.

The
Deserted Island
Theory

This is a letter from Your Nightly Nelson explaining The Deserted Island Theory:

I think this one also came from my buddy Steve Molnar.

Since I have been taking some flack about being one-sided in my letters, I am going to attempt being an equal opportunity offender. Since I am a man and my experiences are with women, I will be writing in reference to the fairer sex. In this particular letter, The Deserted Island Theory will also apply to a man. If you are a woman, as you read this excerpt, you can substitute the word "man" for "woman" and the same meaning will apply.

Here is The Deserted Island Theory.

Whenever someone is stranded on a deserted island or stranded anywhere (say stuck in a bar or a crappy party), they will resort to any measure to survive.

Let's study the situation of a boring party. There are a lot of people at this party, but there is only one person from the opposite sex. Here is where the "man/woman" substitution can be implemented by the way.

First of all, nothing is worse for a guy than being stuck at a sword fight or a helmet fest with only one woman in the room. What is even worse is that the woman is average looking. If you saw her anywhere else, you probably wouldn't hit on her.

But since she is the only woman in the room, your priorities change.

Yes guys, for the first time in your life, looks will not matter. Whoever this woman is, she will now become the best-looking thing in the room. She will be the star, she holds the cards and she knows it.

Every man will be forced to compete over her. Chances are she will give out her phone number to someone. She could also easily apply the One Mile-One Hour Theory.

Why do we call the aforementioned situation The Deserted Island Theory?

Here is a hypothetical situation. There are a bunch of people stranded on an island. There is only one coconut, and it isn't in the best condition. I guarantee that it will still get a lot of attention when stomachs start rumbling.

This is a letter from Your Nightly Nelson.

Nobody Don't Want Nothin' That Nobody Else Don't Want

This is a letter from Your Nightly Nelson explaining to you that, Nobody Don't Want Nothin' That Nobody Else Don't Want:

That phrase was brought to me during one of the broadcasts of *1-800-TALK-SHIT*, by J. Thomas. In his immortal words he said, "Nobody Don't Want Nothin' That Nobody Else Don't Want."

That rings true for all things, especially the opposite sex. Let's look at this from a man's point of view. Think about it. If you can't get a date, it probably means that you are not going to get a date any time soon.

This can be equated to being employed versus being unemployed. When you have a job, everyone out there is offering you a job. When you are looking for a job, you can't seem to get any offers. Basically you aren't wanted and nobody else is going to want you.

Therefore the phrase, "Nobody Don't Want Nothin' That Nobody Else Don't Want", applies.

This leads me to part two of this letter:

"Bait".

Yes, bait. We have all used it. For clarification, bait is different from a wingman.

Many people confuse the two. A wingman is supposed to take the other girl away from her friend so that you can hit on her. A good wingman will also dive on the grenade for you, no questions asked.

Bait is having a good-looking female buddy that is cool with hanging out with you. She can be in The Circle Of Friends or not. But if she is in The Circle Of Friends she will be more cooperative and effective.

You have yourself some bait. Here is how it works. You are hanging out with your female buddy. Women look at you and say, "What does he have? He has a woman with him."

In other words, you are gainfully employed.

Women will see you as a little bit more harmless (hopefully) because you have a woman with you. (For deeper understanding go to the chapter Pathetic Men in Packs.) If you are able to talk to other women, your female buddy will enhance your credibility and raise your stock price by talking you up as a trustworthy individual.

It's a very simple equation. A couple of guys hanging out with a woman equal a couple of fun guys that seem pretty cool.

You will now be wanted. If you are seen with a woman, you can't be that bad.

Remember: alone = bad

You now have a remedy for the dreaded, "Nobody Don't Want Nothin' That Nobody Else Don't Want".

This is a letter from Your Nightly Nelson.

You Must Always Have a Good Wingman

This is a letter from Your Nightly Nelson concerning a good wingman:

Let's define the wingman. A wingman is the guy or girl that keeps the lesser good-looking person busy while you talk to the one that you want. For brevity we will now talk about the person you want as "A" and the lesser good-looking person as "B".

Here is the usual scenario. You are out and you see someone ("A") that you are interested in. Chances are "A" has a friend "B".

Note that women never go out alone.

Sometimes there are even "Cs" and "Ds", but we will discuss that under the multiple wingmen, full squadron or platoon scenario.

You and a friend are out and you want "A". However, "B" can stand in the way from you getting "A". So basically your wingman has to entertain "B", until you can close the sale. It's easy in concept, but are you willing to go though with it?

Here are some pre-game options that you may want to think about.

Before you venture out, determine how well you know your wingman. Will he or she "dive on the grenade" or "take one for the team"? Is he or she willing to make a "sacrifice fly" so you can get a man to home plate? You need to talk about this before you try this maneuver.

Make sure your wingman is willing to find his or her own way home. Make sure they are willing to dive on the grenade, not just talk game and then back out on you at the critical moment.

You should already have a system in place. Know thy territory and know thy limits. Talk about how much alcohol it will take and what is the maximum you are willing to "Clock in At". Also, define your "A" immediately to your wingman, so neither of you are chasing the same target. You must have a plan. Battles and wars are not won without a plan.

Never underestimate "B"! Especially when it comes to women, "B" can ruin things very quickly for you. Why? Women stick together. Men don't care.

Even the hardest nut can be cracked with the proper method. Humor and alcohol are your two best weapons.

The multiple wingmen, full squadron or platoon scenario:

If there are some "C's" and "D's", make sure you have enough company in the platoon or squadron to do the job. Make sure they are willing to dive on the grenade or take one for the team. Are they willing to make a sacrifice fly so that you can get a man to home plate? If squad members are not available, make sure your wingman can take out all others with cover fire or cross-fire. Also make sure you have larger weapons in your arsenal, like pulling other friends from the periphery to use as allies.

In all military maneuvers, you must trust your wingman, and your wingman must never leave you during battle.

This is a letter from Your Nightly Nelson.

LNBC
Rules
of
Engagement

This is a letter from Your Nightly Nelson concerning the LNBC:

The LNBC or the famous acronym for the "Late Night Booty Call" is that little bit of sex that you keep on the side in case all else fails. The LNBC is much like those defibrillators that they put in gyms, churches or the workplace. Only to be used in case of emergency!

If you plan to evoke the LNBC, there are sets of rules or guidelines that are to be followed, or as the military likes to call them: Rules of Engagement.

1. You must have mutual agreement between both parties.

2. The other party must be in a radius of no more than fifteen miles of your present location. (If you have been drinking, it can become an expensive cab ride.)

3. You must have the most readily available contact number for the other party.

4. You have exhausted all means and must have had every door shut in your face throughout the course of the evening while trying to find sex through traditional courses of action.

5. Both parties have a mutual agreement that neither party has to consent to snuggling or talking after sex.

6. Both parties have a mutual agreement that one or the other's party is not responsible for breakfast, coffee or offering a ride back to the other party's permanent location.

7. Both parties must not be engaged in another LNBC for at least six hours.

If you follow these simple rules of engagement, your LNBC will be a fun and rewarding experience.

This is a letter from Your Nightly Nelson.

The
Five-Man
Offense

This is a letter from Your Nightly Nelson giving you the official rules of The Five-Man Offense:

"The Five-Man Offense" is another flaw in man's behavior. This particular letter has a contribution by Fred M. of *Sports and More*. He appears on *Nelson at Nite*.

The Five-Man Offense or "five-men out wide" can be best described as the old run and shoot that the Houston Oilers used to run when Warren Moon was quarterback. You don't have a fullback or tight end blocking for you. You're also not trying to be patient and run the ball; it's total player style. You're just winging it down field in hopes that it will lead to a quick score.

When a man plays The Five-Man Offense, he has to drop back in the pocket alone and unprotected. This translates to a man who is just hitting on any woman that walks by. Basically, he's just throwing the ball all of the time. There's a good chance that the ball is going to be picked off and intercepted. It equates to getting blown off about 99% of the time. But there's always the chance that he has a man open down field, makes the completion and scores.

Getting picked off a lot can lead to run backs and good field position for the other team. This is also a quick way to lose a game.

The opposite of The Five-Man Offense is Ball Control Offense: taking your time, being extra cautious, and handing off the ball on third down, just so you don't throw an interception. Talk to one woman at a time and don't pick the whole club. Keep the ball on the ground and let the running back have a shot at the glory.

I have a rebuttal from J. Thomas, my other half of the radio show *1-800-TALK-SHIT*. Here it is:

"I'm not so sure that The Five-Man Offense is the most effective. In my limited experience a reverse or double reverse is the most effective play. Note that the defense needs to be distracted by alcohol or a big sign that says huge W-2. Then while she's concentrating on the W-2 etc., the offense can lob a pass onto the other side of the field and before she knows it--she's waking up and you've scored."

Some people call this cheating and underhanded.

Those people are alone!

I don't care what they look like…they are alone.

Ethics will keep you cold and lonely on a Friday night! Don't believe me. Ask the next honest, nice, ethical guy you see how many times he's scored in the last six months.

Exactly!

You could try keeping the ball on the ground and running up the middle or even a screen pass but your yardage will be limited because you'll never get past her front line. (Her friends. They run in packs you know). A direct pass over the middle will get picked off by her Lawrence Taylor led defense--the cock-blocking best friend who always says "no" to the friend that always has something going on.

The reverse or better yet double reverse is the best way or the only way to score.

The defense rests.

This is a letter from Your Nightly Nelson.

Seat Up,
Seat Down

This is a letter from Your Nightly Nelson concerning the position of the toilet seat:

No other subject and I mean no other subject, causes more controversy in the household than the position of the toilet seat.

For the life of me, I can't understand why women want it down. Of course, the argument being, that women want to sit and land on a toilet seat and not the porcelain ring of the toilet bowl. I can understand the problem at 3:00 a.m. when the bathroom is dark, but I will give you a work-around for this problem in a few paragraphs.

As men, we have been trained as little boys to put the seat up. If not, we would catch hell from the women in the house. This is where the confusion begins. Remember that men have one-track minds. We can only do one thing at a time. We leave the seat up in case we have to come back in and use the toilet again.

We men are trained well. We put the seat up so that we don't soil it for women. Good deed done. A woman is happy. Then the woman gets mad because the seat is up when she uses the bathroom.

Men now have done something bad.

Men are then confused.

Seat up, Seat down. Why is it my problem? It isn't. I live alone.

Now, to get back to the work-around. We can put LED lights on the toilet that show red when the seat is up and green when the seat is down. That way no one has to turn on the lights at 3:00 a.m.

This is a letter from Your Nightly Nelson.

X. Afterthoughts

The Ten-Minute Relaxation CD/MP3

I wanted to take a page and tell you about a product called The Ten-Minute Relaxation CD/MP3.

The Ten-Minute Relaxation CD/MP3 allows you to relax in ten minutes via guided relaxation to refresh the mind, body and spirit. The Ten-Minute Relaxation CD/MP3 also contains nature sounds so that you can relax to the sounds of the ocean, a tropical rainforest, babbling brook, or even an oscillating desk fan. If you follow the guided commands, you will relax. This CD/MP3 is a form of self-hypnosis where you are simply asked by a narrative voice to give yourself permission to relax, thus leaving you in control. You can bring yourself out of this relaxation any time, just by willing it. You will then be alert and vibrant with no side effects at any time.

These CDs/MP3s have "waking commands" to bring you back from your relaxation, or you can ignore these commands and use the CD/MP3 to help you fall asleep. The audio also has positive affirmations to help you grow and be who YOU want to be. You can also add your own personal positive affirmations when asked to do so. Learn how to make your own positive affirmations by downloading a free MP3.

The CD/MP3 also contains ambient nature sounds mixed with narration and a subliminal narrative track accompanied by nature sounds.

Finally, there are thirty minutes of nature sounds that you can use as background sound while you work, sleep, or just meditate. If you suffer from tinnitus, the ambient sounds can give you some relief so that you can sleep.

You can find these downloads at:

www.tenminuterelaxationcd.com

or

www.cdbaby.com/Artist/NelsonMay.

Active
Darwinism

Active Darwinism is a movement started by yours truly.

Why?

We need to get stupid people out of the gene pool. Charles Darwin was the scientist that laid the foundations of the theory of evolution. He also talked about survival of the fittest.

We simply shouldn't allow stupid people to have children. Yes, let the weak go extinct and let the strong survive. How you go about this is your choice, although I condone violence in any form.

By the way, you are allowed to carry guns in this country. I say that because I simply have respect for the Second Amendment.

Active Darwinism: for more information check out:

www.activedarwinism.com.

Nelson at Nite

Nelson at Nite is the TV show that I talked about in my foreword. I wanted to see if I could make a half-hour talk show and air it on cable access. I was able to pull it off!

When I went into film, I didn't have the time to do *Nelson at Nite* any longer. Later, I was able to set up a studio in my house and broadcast it on YouTube.

We ran 14 shows, and then I started working again.

I hope to get *Nelson at Nite* back on a website near you!

In the meantime, please visit:

www.nelsonatnite.com.

Autobiography

Nelson May grew up just outside of Pittsburgh in Rochester, PA. He graduated from UNC Charlotte with a bachelor's degree in Microbiology. Although his parents wanted him to go into broadcasting school, he wanted to go to medical school and study cardio-pulmonary surgery. After graduation, Nelson was offered a job reporting traffic from an airplane. He started working part-time at local radio stations until finally landing his dream job at a local NPR affiliate. WFAE 90.7 FM was playing contemporary jazz at the time and sometimes Nelson spent 40+ hours a week on the air.

To go a new direction and use his biology degree, Nelson taught 8th and 9th grade science and physics for a few months. He then decided to leave teaching and started a mobile DJ business while still working at NPR. Within that time frame, he was offered a part-time job selling sports memorabilia. For the next five years, Nelson developed his on air skills, mobile DJ abilities and sales strengths.

In 2000, he decided to leave the corporate environment and become a voice actor. He made a home studio and with help from his father built an impressive sound booth. Voice acting was very lucrative until Hurricane Katrina hit. Then gas prices began to rise in the United States. This economic stress put a lot of Nelson's smaller voice clients out of business. Seeing the writing on the wall, Nelson enrolled in a few film classes at the local community college to learn film and editing.

He started working on commercials and eventually was trained in the position of Video Assist. Nelson worked on commercials for the next few years while still doing one of two live shows left on WFAE called *Nightscapes*.

As his film career began to mature, Nelson had to leave radio to devote his energy to film full time. After editing a golf show for two years, he decided to enter the construction side of filmmaking.

Nelson was a Propmaker on *The Hunger Games* and Showtime's *Homeland*. He also worked at a cinema rental company called Cinelease and slowly became an Electrician. His additional film credits include *Iron Man 3* and *Homeland* (Season 2). Nelson also taught voice acting at various broadcasting schools and taught Public Speaking for Duke University's Certificate Program for Non-Profit Management.

Letters from Your Nightly Nelson is to be the ultimate "backup career" in case everything else falls apart.

Nelson May loves the film industry and will always work in some aspect of film and TV. If *Letters From Your Nightly Nelson* takes off, Nelson will follow the path and let it run its course.

This is a blank page for you to write down any comments or thoughts about this book. Please find something to write, since this extra page is costing me money to print.

This is a second blank page for you to write down any comments or thoughts about this book. Please find something to write, since this extra page is costing me money to print.

www.ingramcontent.com/pod-product-compliance
Lightning Source LLC
Chambersburg PA
CBHW070819120626
46556CB00002B/570